BEYOND THE LIGHTS

STORIES

RYAN SHOEMAKER

NO RECORD PRESS
2018

NO RECORD PRESS
www.norecordpress.com

Shoemaker, Ryan
Beyond the Lights
Ryan Shoemaker.

ISBN: 978-0-9835860-2-9

Cover design by Eric Obenauf
Interior layout by Eliza Wood-Obenauf

Publisher's notes:

This is entirely a work of fiction.

The stories in this collection were first published elsewhere: *McSweeney's Internet Tendency*, "A Stay-at-Home Dad Documents His Sex Life on a Fitbit—Here's What Happened"; *Bull: Men's Fiction*, "Journal of a Stay-at-Home Dad"; *Booth*, "A Letter to Daniel LaRusso, the Karate Kid"; *Monkeybicycle*, "Brigham Kimball:Mormon Missionary Extraordinaire"; *Monarch Review*, "I Reject Your Rejection"; *Grist*, "The Crossing"; *Santa Monica Review*, "Beyond the Lights"; *Silk Road Review* and *Dialogue: A Journal of Mormon Thought*, "The Righteous Road"; *Dialogue: A Journal of Mormon Thought*, "Great Heights"; *Juked*, "Lost in Furniture Land"; *The Fiction Desk* and *Hawai'i Review*, "After All the Fun We Had"; *Weber: The Contemporary West*, "Our Students"; *Concho River Review*, "This Same Darkness"

Printed in the United States of America.

For Jen. Our story is still my favorite.

For Tom and Aimee. The words. Always the words.

For Joe, my fellow traveler.

"No people are uninteresting."
—Yevgeny Yevtushenko, "People"

"I worked. I turned over money. Somebody gave me a cat. It shat in a box under the sink and filled the house with a graveyard stink."
—T.C. Boyle, "The 100 Faces of Death, Volume IV"

"And it seemed as though in a little while the solution would be found, and then a new and splendid life would begin; and it was clear to both of them that they had still a long, long way to go, and that the most complicated and difficult part of it was only just beginning."
—Anton Chekhov, "The Lady with the Dog"

Table of Contents

Husbands, Fathers, and Sons

A Stay-at-Home Dad Documents His Sex Life on a Fitbit—Here's What Happened

For dinner, make Lisa's favorites: the Southwestern kale and black bean salad and the organic chicken soup recipes I found on Pinterest. But thoughtfully leave out the black beans since Lisa complained that they make her gassy at her early-morning hot yoga class.

Heart rate: 81 bpm

Set the table with the wineglasses we use only for Thanksgiving and the silver candelabra with hanging crystal hearts I bought on sale last week at Bed Bath & Beyond.

Heart rate: 86 bpm

All through dinner, give Lisa smoldering, seductive looks from across the table, even when Piper smears chewed kale on the wall and Caleb farts loudly while picking raisins from the Southwestern salad with his fingers.

Heart rate: 74 bpm

Wash the dishes, scour the countertops and stove. Spend an extra five minutes scrubbing the spinach and chia seed residue from Lisa's Vitamix Turboblend 4500.

Heart rate: 91 bpm

Bathe the children, get them in jammies, read a bedtime story about an ambitious rooster that dreams of becoming an astronaut. Tuck the kiddies into bed and sing "Itsy Bitsy Spider" five times until they fall into a peaceful slumber.

Heart rate: 94 bpm

Stand in our bedroom doorway as Lisa changes into satin boxers and a tight tank top. Casually mention the healthy dinner, spotless kitchen, bathed children, and extra-clean Vitamix Turboblend 4500. Wait for Lisa to offer a sexual reward for the many well-done domestic tasks. When Lisa offers nothing, take a more direct approach: ask Lisa if tonight is convenient for sexual relations. Remind Lisa it's been two weeks since our last coupling on October 20th.

Heart rate: 96 bpm

Do a vigorous fist pump in the hallway after Lisa checks her phone for any morning meetings, glances at her watch, and then consents to sexual relations.

Heart rate: 98 bpm

Prepare for our amorous encounter: brush and floss teeth, apply Acqua di Gio to neck and earlobes, scrub my private parts vigorously with a hot washrag in case Lisa feels wild tonight, like last February when she drank too many margaritas at her book club and actually suggested we make love on our bedroom floor!

Heart rate: 87 bpm

Lie on the bed and wait for Lisa to finish the final chapter of *Vampire Chronicles: Volume 1*. Give more smoldering, seductive looks and hope that Lisa sees the enormous bulge protruding from my flannel jammies.

Heart rate: 66 bpm

Listen patiently as Lisa recounts the entire plot of *Vampire Chronicles: Volume 1*. Nod eagerly and hope my energetic headshaking disperses the Acqua di Gio and puts Lisa in a sexy mood.

Heart rate: 83 bpm

Strip off my flannel jammies and fold them neatly before setting them on the nightstand. Nibble Lisa's earlobes. Massage her left butt cheek.

Heart rate: 101 bpm

Jump out of the bed quickly when Lisa gives a loud, nonsexual gasp because she might have heard a strange noise in the kitchen.

Heart rate: 114 bpm

Tiptoe naked through the house clutching Piper's tee-ball bat. Check the door locks. Peek through the living room drapes and see two cats, bathed in milky moonlight, humping on the front lawn. Stand there a moment and envy the humping cats.

Heart rate: 110 bpm

Return to the room to assure Lisa that all is well. Wait patiently as she finishes the first chapter of *Vampire Chronicles: Volume 2*.

Heart rate: 74 bpm

Massage Lisa's breasts and trill playfully into her ear about how I can't wait to read the entire *Vampire Chronicles* series—after I finish scrapbooking our summer vacation to Disneyworld and Gatorland.

Heart rate: 99 bpm

Quickly dismount Lisa when the bedroom door swings open and Caleb's standing there. Walk Caleb to his room and promise pony rides, inflatable castles, a large Slurpee, and a bag of Sour Patch Kids if he'll just stay the hell in bed. When Caleb asks why I'm naked, say very calmly that Daddy fell out of his jammies.

Heart rate: 109 bpm

Return to Lisa's breasts, but wait as she taps out a concerned text to a coworker about the subpar quinoa and arugula salad she ordered for lunch. Look at a picture of the salad on Instagram and agree with Lisa that, indeed, some of the arugula looks rather wilted.

Heart rate: 66 bpm

Kiss Lisa passionately on the lips. Lick her right earlobe. Moan as Lisa uses her fingernails to firmly massage a small spot over my left shoulder blade. Feel that Lisa must really be turned on because usually she's never into foreplay.

Heart rate: 105 bpm

Suddenly realize that Lisa's picking at a large blackhead on my back! Listen patiently as she criticizes the Suave Refreshing Splash Shower Gel I've used since college and then extols her Chanel Coco Bath Bar for its pleasing fragrance and invigorating moisturizers. Promise Lisa that I'll take better care of my skin by drinking more water, applying sunscreen daily, and using a body soap with natural oils.

Heart rate: 65 bpm

Lightly bite Lisa's elbow as I affectionately rub her kneecaps, but stop when she realizes that she forgot to take her birth control pill. Listen attentively as she says there's no way in hell she'll ever put on all that baby weight again and wear those hideous maternity pants with the elastic waistband.

Heart rate: 103 bpm

Sprint to bathroom for Lisa's pill and a glass of water.

Heart rate: 113 bpm

Return to bedroom to find Lisa in her Brookstone sleeping mask, snoring loudly.

Heart rate: 89 bpm

Walk to bathroom and rummage under sink until I find the worn 2011 Victoria's Secret Fall Fashion catalog I stashed in a box of old washrags and luffa sponges. Turn to the "Satin Indulgences" section with the busty brunette who looks like Anne Hathaway in *The*

Dark Knight Rises. Imagine Catwoman/Anne Hathaway straddling the Batpod in tight black leather and that sexy feline mask.

Heart rate: 104 bpm

Suddenly notice the two-page living room spread in the open Crate and Barrel catalog that I had been browsing during my morning bowel movement. My heart begins to pound and my face flushes with the sight of all that gorgeous furniture, the buxom Rochelle leather sofa, the creamy decorative pillows, and the beautifully erect Tribeca floor lamp. Close my eyes. Bite my lip. Fantasize about what it would be like to caress the sofa's supple full-grain leather and the pillows' luscious silken thread, to turn that Tribeca floor lamp on.

Heart rate: 150 bpm

Journal of a Stay-at-Home Dad: June 20, 2009

5:00 a.m. Working on a screenplay about a Jamaican pigeon blown from his tropical paradise by a Category 5 hurricane and dumped into New York City's Upper East Side. Writing in garage still. Have grown accustomed to the flimsy card-table "desk" wedged between the lawnmower and the stacked washer/dryer. Lately, been considering a more personal screenplay about a laid-off investment banker whose wife returns to work. Ex-investment banker becomes Mr. Stay-at-Home Dad. Tragedy, comedy, romance, horror?

5:45 a.m. Through garage window, see a gray, mud-smeared pickup truck across the street. Been there all night. Somebody inside. A shadowed figure. Strange. Will call police if the truck is still there tomorrow.

7:30 a.m. Vanessa leaves. Tap-tap of stiletto heels on porch. Her note on kitchen counter says:

Dale,

It'll be a late night. My team's finalizing the presentation for next year's fiscal strategy. I can taste the promotion! Remember, Zoe needs more lean protein, and no sugar for Skyler. And only give them sandwiches on sprouted-wheat bread!!!!!!! Don't forget their gummy vitamins, either.

Love,
Vanessa

P.S. I can't wait to get a piece of your furry ass when I get home.

7:32 a.m. Wad the note into a tight ball and punt it across the kitchen. For breakfast, make the kids hash browns, bacon, and scrambled eggs with Hollandaise sauce. Hollandaise recipe Jill gave me. Will tell her how the kids greedily licked the sauce from their plates and fingers.

8:30 a.m. Check email to see if playgroup is still at McCambridge Park. See an email from Jill. Might be the deviled eggs recipe she promised. No.

Dale,

Nolan told me last night that he doesn't like us hanging out together, even if it's just playdates for Zoe and Madison. Not that he thinks you aren't trustworthy or have bad intentions. He just wants me to hang out with women when he's not around. Sorry.

Warmly,
Jill

P.S. Thanks for the crème brûlée recipe. Amazing!

P.P.S. Actually, Nolan's really pissed off at you.

9:00 a.m. Shocked! Email all I think about as we head out the door for playgroup. And just as we pile into the minivan, the shadowed figure steps from the gray pickup truck across street. Nolan! Six feet five, steel-toed boots, muddy jeans, fluorescent orange construction vest, hard hat, three days' stubble on his face. He wields an axe handle. "You stay the hell away from my wife," he shouts, stabbing the axe handle in my direction. "You hear me, Donaldson?"

Nolan's back in the truck, gunning the engine, spinning the tires, throwing out a grayish pall of diesel smoke and vaporized rubber that lingers around us. He's halfway down the block before I turn to kids. My heart pounds against my shirt. Terrified but ready to comfort these tender souls, ready to explain the brutal adult world to these innocent minds, ready to tout the nobility of a higher moral road and the unsung glories of pacifism. But Skyler's giggling wildly, jumping up and down and making engine noises, screaming for more "vroom-vroom" and smoke. Zoe stands there with a sad face and weepy eyes. I kneel to console her, to wipe away the tears. She says, "Why can't you have a cool truck like Madison's daddy?" Then she stomps into the van and gives me the stink-eye all the way to the park.

9:15 a.m. Playgroup moms chat about childbirth, cookie recipes, self-help books, and handsome vampires. In no mood to talk. Just swing Skyler and think about Jill and her brutish husband. Does Nolan know Jill's dream of becoming a trapeze artist and a lion tamer? Does he know she's writing a young-adult novel about a girl who flees a dead-end Midwestern town to join the circus? How will I reply to Jill's email?

Steve, the other playgroup dad, is at the picnic tables talking with mothers, telling some story about how his adopted daughter Emily barfed into a potted plant at a family funeral last summer. All the mothers laugh. Steve laughs. He puts his hands on their shoulders, touches their elbows, gives hugs. I envy Steve, because he's gay, because he can go out for coffee with these women. Not a threat. No bad intentions. Lucky Steve.

9:30 a.m. Phone buzzes. Text from Vanessa:

Don't forget to give the kids their teaspoon of flaxseed after lunch. I can't wait to nibble your ankles tonight. Grrrrrrrrrrr!

I delete text.

12:00 p.m. Run errands: kids' dentist appointments, pick up dry cleaning, wash van, buy worm pills for Buttons, get Skyler's ear medicine. Home for lunch and naps.

3:00 p.m. Grocery store. Push kids in a cart shaped like a cartoonish racecar. No lean meat and veggies for dinner tonight. Vanessa has an irrational fear of simple carbohydrates. Believes a single bite of refined pasta will turn her thighs into lardy blobs. Grab two boxes of Kraft Macaroni and Cheese and a package of Ballpark Franks. Kids cheer loudly.

I'm surprised to see Jill at the end of the aisle. Follow and call her name. She doesn't turn. I follow her to the dairy aisle. Nervous. Don't know what to say, but must say something. Touch Jill's elbow. She turns. It's not Jill! It's some college kid with long hair and a goatee. Apologize and keep walking.

5:00 p.m. Make dinner. Skyler grabs my leg and giggles. He says, "Daddy, you comfy and toasty." Zoe draws a picture of me smiling in what looks like a billowing, sequined prom dress and a sparkling tiara. Still, a good picture. Hang it on the refrigerator and tell myself: These are the moments. This is what I would miss.

7:00 p.m. Bath. Pajamas. A bedtime story about an ambitious rooster who dreams of flying south for the winter but learns to accept his flightless life. The end.

8:00 p.m. Clean kitchen. Bury macaroni and cheese box and hotdog package in the bottom of the trashcan, under some mushy cantaloupe rinds and coffee grounds.

8:45 p.m. Sit at the computer. How to reply to Jill's email? I type:

Jill,

Time will pass, but I will never forget. So sad, this parting, so sad. Farewell, my beloved friend. Farewell! Farewell!

9:00 p.m. Delete the draft, then shut down the computer. Won't reply to Jill's email. Can never speak to Jill again. Will only and always stare at her from a distance at ballet and piano recitals, tee-ball games and school carnivals.

9:15 p.m. My head and lower back ache. Take Ambien and crawl into bed. Think of Jill. Know I love Jill. Yes, I love Jill. But will never reveal my fantasy of us living at high altitude in a rustic log cabin, baking bread, churning butter, and curing hams in a smoke house. I imagine our children frolicking in homespun clothes, smiling as they swing in pine trees and skip through flowered mountain meadows. Never to be.

10:00 p.m. Front door lock turns. Hold my breath and listen to the tap-tap of stiletto heels on the wooden floor. The sound terrifies me. The bedroom door opens. Vanessa's there, looming, backlit by the hallway light. I feign sleep and make sleepy sounds. Only want sleep.

"Where's my little man?" Vanessa says. "Is my little man ready for some yum-yum?"

Try to imagine serrated, snow-dusted peaks, pure mountain air, and clear water boiling over smooth stones, but see only a lost pigeon, a laid-off investment banker, and a sad, flightless rooster staring at the sky. And then as Vanessa ravages me, I think: *Jill, Jill, Jill.*

A Letter to Daniel LaRusso, the Karate Kid

Dear Daniel,

Good talking with you at the All-Valley Karate Championships. What a story you have! Inspiring. Seriously. The stuff movies are made of. Consider me a big fan. I don't know, maybe I saw something of myself in you, the lanky underdog trying to get his footing in that first match and then finding his stride, fighting, really, for his life and not just some trophy or title.

But even with all that heart, Daniel, I had my doubts. Really. I mean, anyone would, right? Fact is, you're this skinny Italian kid from Newark who took a couple karate classes at the YMCA and then got bamboozled into doing these really awful chores for Mr. Miyagi. Second fact: by the time you got to the championship match, those Cobra Kai had unmercifully wrung you out, and Johnny Lawrence, tempered by all those years of practiced roundhouses and knuckle push-ups in the dojo, was just warming to the task of wiping the mats with you. And you, hobbling around like a ninety-year-old man, practically crippled, and then carted off on a stretcher.

By that point, I thought best case scenario was you on a morphine drip in Valley Presbyterian ICU. Worst case scenario? Maybe you in a body bag. Then you were suddenly back in the arena, all smiles as you waved to the crowd.

Then that awesome crane kick to Johnny's jaw. And then Ali running out in that sexy purple miniskirt and those white knee-high socks, and your mom there, too, the maternal relief on her face, because all those worries and uncertainties about this California move—the crappy swimming pool, the mysterious ass-whoppings, your strange relationship with an old Japanese guy—have vanished. And of course Mr. Miyagi, in that totally 70s retro shirt with the huge pointed collar, grinning slyly like the proud father he always wanted to be, because he imparted his ancient karate wisdom, taught you all those cool life lessons and, at the same time, secretly got you to fix up his old bachelor pad by the railroad tracks.

And when it couldn't get any better, Johnny, your arch enemy, the guy who kicked your ass all over town and even once at the beach, now humbled and repentant, hands you that huge gold trophy and tells you you're all right. The adoring crowd, the praise of friends, family, and strangers, the rich girl you love toweling the sweat from your brow—what a moment! But don't kid yourself, Daniel, into thinking you and Ali will live happily ever after up in the Hollywood Hills.

Reality is, in the end, you don't get Ali. Johnny does. Sure, you'll be the big man on campus for the rest of the year, the working man's hero for Freddy and all the other Reseda kids who had to endure Johnny's titty-twisters and atomic-wedgies since middle school. On weekends, you and Ali will cruise the Pacific Coast Highway in your vintage Ford Super Deluxe convertible to roast hot dogs and kick a soccer ball around Zuma Beach. Or you'll eat pizza and make out in the dark comfort of Ali's home theater while watching *Revenge of the Nerds*. And Ali's parents will be cool with you, even though you don't have Johnny's moneyed, Anglo pedigree, and nothing even close to that perfect crescent of corn-silk blond hair that floats on his forehead. They'll be cool with you, at least until the end of summer, because this will be a rich cultural experience for their daughter, much safer than a study abroad to Haiti or Burundi to see how the ninety-nine percent live. Maybe, they hope, Ali will even turn her slumming into a really cool personal essay for her freshman composition class at USC. They know you two won't last.

Why? Because Ali will go off to USC in her dad's old Mercedes coupe, and when she calls, she'll go on and on about rush week and all-night keggers on Greek Row and how her roommate, Samantha, is dating William Shatner's nephew. And you'll have no idea what the hell she's talking about, because you're still living in the South Sea Apartments with your mom, slapping pizzas together full time at the Domino's in Burbank and taking a few evening classes at West Los Angeles College.

Now and then you'll meet up with Ali and her college friends at Zuma Beach, skinny you, still stinking of Canadian bacon, in cut-off Levi's and a muscle shirt, with a smear of marinara sauce on your left earlobe. And when you bounce a soccer ball on your knee and suggest a quick game, they'll look at you like you just pissed in their vanilla frappuccinos.

Soon, Ali won't come home much on weekends and will seldom return your calls. When you do go out, her mind will be elsewhere, certainly not on the new windmill hazard at Golf N' Stuff or the white-knuckle drop of the water slides you planned for a Saturday date. You'll hear from Freddy, who's busing tables weekends at the Woodland Hills Country Club, that he's seen Ali there with Johnny, dancing, lip-locking, and then disappearing into the night on the back of his Ninja 600R.

In a rage, still wearing your red, white and blue Domino's uniform, you'll gun it down to USC in your vintage car and there find Ali and her friends hanging out on the grass in the McCarthy Quad. When you wave at Ali, her face will flush a deep red and then she'll look away and pretend you're not there. A blond frat boy you remember from the beach will say, "Hey, Daniel, where the hell's our pizza?" And everyone, including Ali, will laugh hysterically. And like you did at the country club when you had goulash smeared all over those sharp, white jeans, you'll run.

On the way home you'll stop at a bar in Van Nuys and drink beer after beer thanks to the fake ID Freddy gave you for your eighteenth birthday. And when some leathered biker from Tujunga makes fun of the way you say *water* and *over there*, you'll raise your arms and leg into crane kick position and then fall on your ass when you slip in a puddle of Old Milwaukee. For the second time that night, you'll run.

Pizzas you make by the hundreds, general eds at the community college, your mom's awful scrambled eggs each morning, and the annoying way she blabs on and on about your gorgeous baby browns to make you feel better about yourself. You'll spiral into a dark depression. Mr. Miyagi won't be any help. When he's not fishing for striped bass at Castaic Lake, he'll be mentoring another at-risk teenager, some Armenian kid with a harelip who's getting the bejesus wonked out of him every morning at the bus stop.

In bed at night you'll stare up at the tough-looking trophy on your bookcase and try to recall every sensation of your victory at the All-Valley Karate Championships, the crowd's deafening approval, Ali's tender encouragement, and the solid, fleshy weight of foot connecting to jaw. Still lying in bed, you'll practice the old moves: wax on, wax off; sand the floor; paint the fence; crane kick. Your mom will hear the bed banging against the wall and worry that your deep depression has led you to the mortal sin of self-pleasure.

But we're fighters, Daniel. We've always been fighters. A deadbeat dad. Smoky apartment buildings with blistering paint and crumbling stucco. Wheezing clunkers. The shame of thrift store clothes and free lunches. All we've ever done is fight.

While working full time as a manager at Domino's, you'll finish your associate's degree in plumbing technology and start an apprenticeship with a construction company in Pacoima. You'll move out of your mom's apartment. You'll trade in the Ford Super Deluxe for a Honda with good gas mileage and plenty of trunk space. You'll grow up, Daniel. You'll move on.

Still, you'll often wander the dimly lit arcade at Golf N' Stuff and think of Ali, imagining how different your life might have been if you were one of those kids from the Hills. And then one night the girl collecting prize tickets behind the counter will say to you in a thick Jersey accident, "Hey, why so depressed, paisano?" You'll laugh and stop to talk. Her name will be Vivian Giordano, and she'll be staying with her aunt in Canoga Park for the year, saving money for beauty school when she returns to Jersey City. She won't have Ali's blonde hair and soft curves in all the right places, but she'll love you, even if you weren't All-Valley Karate Champion but just some guy with a used Honda and a one-bedroom apartment in Tarzana. And she'll love you, Daniel, even when you drag yourself through the door at the end of a long work day reeking of sewage, long, long after your hair recedes and your cheeks sag into fleshy jowls. And on Saturdays when she's cheering you on from a park bench as you kick a soccer ball through the grass with your son and daughter close behind, you will be a champion.

Daniel, I know how you're feeling. Trust me. I've been there myself, the skinny Italian kid from the other side of town, trophy in hand, punch-drunk from the sweet thrill of victory and the warm embrace of the blonde girl from the Hills. All I'm saying is, don't get too hung up on the pretty girl and the view from the Hills. Though hard to believe, you'll see, Daniel. Even without Ali and the Hills, your life will be better than you ever imagined.

All the best,

Vincent Castellano,
All-Valley Karate Champion, 1975

Brigham Kimball: Mormon Missionary Extraordinaire

Called to Serve

Brigham's mission call, an excerpt: *You are assigned to labor in the Honduras San Pedro Sula Mission. You will prepare to preach the gospel in the Spanish language. . . .*

Brigham's mom, Jackie, pulls a map from top shelf of the coat closet and spreads it across the dining room table. She's on the phone with Grandma Kimball.

"Yes, he just got his call," she yells into the phone. "Honduras. I see it right here on the map. It's in southern Mexico. I'm sure they do, Mom. These days everyone has a washing machine and a microwave."

Brigham dusts off his old junior high Spanish assignments. For dinner, Jackie makes tacos. Brigham's father, John, buys a piñata, which, after dinner, the family blithely pulverizes with a broomstick.

Farewell Talk at Church

Brigham, excerpt from talk: *I echo the words of that mighty prophet, Joseph Smith, who, looking out over his beloved Nauvoo for the last time, said: "I go as a lamb to the slaughter; but I am calm as a summer's morning; I have a conscience void of sin and offense before God, and before all men. I shall die innocent, and it shall be said of me—he was murdered in cold blood."*

Brigham weeps, Jackie weeps, John weeps, Grandma and Grandpa Kimball weep. Aunts, uncles, cousins, nephews, and nieces weep. Brigham's girlfriend, Heather, weeps, friends weep, babies weep. Priests and High Priests sleep. Bishop Sanders eyes his watch and nervously taps his Wingtips. A deacon brings up a fresh box of Kleenex.

Missionary Training Center: Provo, Utah

Savory Salisbury steak, spaghetti with a rich meat sauce, a taco bar. Brigham puts on weight. He devotes himself to learning Spanish. In fact, he never speaks a word of English. Brian Holland, his companion, occasionally forgets Elder Kimball's name.

Airport

Brigham mutters goodbyes in Spanish. "*Voy a convertir el mundo*," he says. He embraces Jackie, embraces John, affectionately shakes Heather's hand. While he's away, Heather promises to plan their wedding.

First Night in Honduras

Fleas, ticks, chiggers, earwigs, gnats, roaches, rats. Bats, beetles, mice, mites, lice. Spitting spiders, jumping spiders, barking spiders, flying spiders. Fire ants, Azteca ants, Parasol ants, Tuxedo ants. Diggers, gougers, itchers, stingers, stabbers.

Serve with Honor

A letter from John, Brigham's father. An excerpt: *Brigham, an honorable mission is the foundation of a successful life. I truly believe that. Too many squander the experience. You might feel it's not in my character to say this, but let me impart some sage advice my father gave me right before I left on my mission. "Son," he said. "Keep your pecker in the birdhouse."*

Brigham's First Baptism

Brigham and Pedro Sanchez wade into the dark, meandering river. Piranhas nip at their heels, crocodiles dismember a yak on the opposite bank, primitive savages beat drums in the distance.

Coming up from the water, Pedro embraces Brigham and intones a high, lispy *Gracias* in his ear. Brigham feels Pedro's hand clamped tightly around his right buttock. "What a strange custom," Brigham thinks.

Altercation

A letter from Brigham's companion, Elder Parker, to Guadalupe Rancho de la Lengua, an excerpt translated from Spanish: *What I wouldn't give to get some distance between me and this new elder. What's his name? Kimball. That's right. Every morning I have to wake up to his chipper voice and that stupid grin on his happy face. I want him to stop shining my shoes. I think I'll scream if he says even one more time with that dreamy look in his eyes, "Elder, these are our days in the history of the church." The only thing that makes life bearable is you, seeing you across the chapel on Sundays, getting your letters. When I'm back in Utah, I'll send you money for a plane ticket. We'll drive up Provo Canyon in my Mustang. We'll eat lunch in a grassy meadow. You can make those cheese empanadas I love.*

Brigham confronts Elder Parker about a romantic letter he finds on the bathroom sink. Parker denies everything. Brigham also expresses concern over Parker's lack of interest in their morning companionship study. "You'll never understand our love," Parker says, and then, right before kicking Brigham in the groin, screams, "Put this in your journal!"

More Companion Problems

An excerpt from one of Brigham's letters to his father: *I just got transferred to a city off the Mosquito Coast called Trujillo. I'm now companions with Elder Ramirez. He's from Caracas and tells me he used to be a cage fighter, but gave it up when he became a Mormon.*

I don't think he quite understands what we're supposed to do as missionaries. He's always trying to sell our investigators these Rolex knock-offs. He has a bunch of them looped around a string he's tied into the lining of his suit jacket, and at the end of a lesson he opens the jacket and makes his pitch. It's quite awkward. Do you think I should speak with Mission President Hurley?

One night Brigham has a mildly erotic dream about Heather. They're in a city he doesn't recognize, sitting in the back of taxi that speeds through empty streets. Inexplicably, they're both dressed in purple leisure suits. Heather delicately kneads the back of Brigham's neck.

And then Brigham's suddenly awoken by the shuffle of naked feet on saltillo tile, a book falling, and the swish of fabric. Through the pale darkness, Brigham watches Ramirez thumbing through his wallet, pulling out crisp dollar bills, ogling Heather's senior picture.

"Elder," Brigham asks, "*Qué estás haciendo*?"

"*Amigo*," Ramirez hisses, and then in a broken, effeminate English says, "The only thing in this world that gives orders is balls." His hair sticks up. His eyes are wild. "*Silenzio, Elder*."

Dear John

Brigham's fiancée, Heather, hasn't written in months. He assumes her heavy course load in Family Science at Brigham Young University must be the cause, and then one day a letter arrives. Instead of emanating the pleasant scent of Heather's Tommy Girl perfume, the letter reeks of dirty diapers.

Heather, excerpt from letter: *It just happened so quickly with Phil. I mean, it was just a group of us watching* The NeverEnding Story, *and Phil and I were crying during all the same scenes, like in the end when Bastian and the Empress are sitting there and she has the last grain of sand from Fantasia in her palm. Everyone got tired of the movie and left, and it was just the two of us, and I was like, "This is my favorite movie of all time," and Phil was like,*

"Yeah, mine too." It was like we were meant to get married. I mean, we love the same movie! It was a sign. Anyway, since I'd already planned our wedding, all I had to do was replace your name with Phil's on the invitations. That's why it happened so quickly. It was crazy. I forgot to write. Forgive me. So have a good mission. There's someone out there for you. I'd write more but I have to feed Lizzy. She's been fussy lately. I think she's getting a diaper rash.

That night Brigham quietly weeps into his pillow.

A Letter from Mission President Hurley

An excerpt: *Elder Kimball, next week I'm sending a new missionary your way, an Elder Casper from Vernon, Utah, fresh from the Missionary Training Center. I'll expect you to train him well. Teach him to preach the gospel with boldness. Teach him Spanish. With increased responsibility come greater blessings.*

Looking over your last letter to me, I see you're contemplating a major in pre-law when you return to BYU. As an attorney, I advise against it. As you see, I'm as big as a house. It came upon me suddenly in my early thirties. Too much sitting in courtrooms and conference rooms, too many lunches at Essex House and Jean Georges, all those billing hours to make partner. I let myself go. I can't even buy pants off the rack anymore. My knees are shot. If I could go back, I'd be a logger or a fisherman or a gentleman farmer. I'd have learned how to cobble shoes. Law is death, Elder! Death and pain and loneliness. I'm a tender soul and they think I'm a monster. Find success serving the Lord, Elder. That's the secret.

A Trainer

Elders Kimball and Casper hike wooded hills, wade sewage-choked streams, knock on doors. They smile. They push pamphlets and the *Book of Mormon* on the unbelieving. They pray for the poor and needy. They implore inactive members to return to church.

One day, a little boy stops them. He's digging in a trash heap. His fingers and cheeks are stained black, and he wears an extra-large T-shirt with *Don't Piss Me Off, Butt-Munch* printed across the chest.

(Conversation with boy translated from Spanish.)

The boy points to Brigham's black nametag. "That's my name, too."

"Your name?" Brigham is baffled. He feels he's missed something.

"Elder," the boy says. He smiles. Strangely, his teeth are white and straight. "Elder's my first name."

Brigham laughs, dropping to one knee in front of the boy. "Elder? And where did you get a name like that?"

The boy stares at his grubby bare feet, suddenly shy. "My mommy said it was my daddy's first name, just like yours. You and my daddy have the same first name. Do you know where he is? I never met him."

Elder Casper grins dumbly as he fumbles through a pocket-sized English/Spanish dictionary. "What's he saying? I caught about a third of it. His father. Is his father interested in hearing our lessons?"

"Let's get out of here," Brigham says.

Brigham's Advice to Elder Casper

Don't drink the water, don't pet the dogs, don't ride horses, don't eat the dried fish, never share a bed with your companion, don't believe any girl who confesses her love for you—and keep your pecker in the birdhouse.

The Triumphant Return Home

Brigham appears at the end of the jetway. His suit is in tatters. He has jock itch and an intestinal parasite. He has about him the smell of the jungle. The camera flashes blind him. He sprints through a paper banner that reads *Well done, good and faithful servant.* All weep.

I Reject Your Rejection

Fiction Editor
The West Coast Review
460 Geary Street, Suite 119
San Francisco, CA 94102

November 5, 2016

Dear Fiction Editor,

I was dismayed yesterday to receive your photocopied, unevenly cut, off-center form letter rejecting my short story "Mountains of Blood," which I sent to your journal on September 15th. The purpose of this letter is to inform you that I reject your rejection.

Perhaps I was too modest in my submission letter, but I'm actually kind of a big deal in the greater Elko, Nevada literary scene. The box in my mom's front yard marked "Kevin's Stories—Free" is nearly always empty by the end of the week. Mrs. Turner, who often takes a story when she passes our house on her morning walk, has told me that my writing is "colorful" and "descriptive." Once she even used the word "poignant." A homeless man everyone knows as Red Beard Willie is also a big fan, grabbing at least half the stories each Wednesday, and though I know he's using them as bedding, or so my friend Chip with the Parks Department tells me, I have no doubt Willie does so to have my sharp prose close by when he wants something to read at night.

You should also know that my fan base extends far beyond Elko. Once, I received an encouraging email from a Nigerian banker named Mr. Buhari, who'd read my story "The Practical Psycho" online at *Literary Gravy* and suggested I self-publish a collection of short fiction with an abandoned sum of ten million dollars from a United Bank of Africa client who died in a horrific plane crash over the French Alps. Unfortunately, since I'd recently been fired from my janitorial position at Home Depot (writing on the job—yes, that's how dedicated I am!), I didn't have the thousand dollars to start a joint bank account with Mr. Buhari so we could access the ten million dollars. My mom wouldn't loan me the money because she thought the whole thing sounded stupid. (Really, I think she was resistant because she resents all the overbearing, emasculating mothers many of my protagonists must nobly fight against in their quest for freedom.) Another time, a Ukrainian woman emailed me to say how she'd absolutely loved a short piece I'd placed online at *Rabid Monkey Slush*. She'd loved the piece so much, in fact, that she was on her way to Elko to discuss the story's dark symbolism and Oedipal themes when a pack of gypsies mugged her in a Munich city park. Hysterical, she emailed me twenty times in two hours to say she needed money to sort out her hotel bill and buy a plane ticket to continue her trip to Elko. Unmoved by this dedicated fan's plight, my mom again refused to loan me the money.

I understand, however, that an artist can't always lean on reputation and past laurels. The work in hand must speak for itself. That's why I encourage you to reread "Mountains of Blood." What about the story's beginning? *Opaque shadows creep toward me through the dishwater light. The fire has burned low. Outside, the sky glows red, and the mountains are blood.* Isn't it clear from these well-wrought lines that Steven, my henpecked protagonist, has just recently bludgeoned his domineering mother to death with a work boot and is now held up in an isolated cabin while the police, or so he suspects, close in on him? And what about the building suspense in these lines? *Frozen with fear, my heart rate picks up. I glance around. The clown painting on the wall has fallen to the ground and cracked.* Can't you see that Steven is actually going insane and that it's not the police who are closing in but the vindictive spirit of the dead mother come to kill him with fear? And what about the superb ending when Steven topples from the balcony while fleeing his mother's ghost and impels himself on the patio umbrella below? How could "Mountains of Blood" not be a perfect fit for your storied, prestigious journal?

I've also considered that perhaps you weren't adequately prepared to appreciate my dark, probing prose. Maybe a writerly habit I've developed to prime the creative pump might be of use to you in your editorial process. In the box accompanying this letter, find a bottle of Poco Loco Especial XXX Tequila. I recommend not eating anything for eight hours and then drinking the whole bottle as quickly as possible. You'll see: in no time the prose will sing and the characters will leap from the page.

Also in the box, please find a photograph of me. It will go nicely with my contributor bio when you publish "Mountains of Blood" in your winter issue. The green tweed jacket, Dunhill pipe, Salvador Dali mustache, and my relaxed pose with one elbow resting on a fire-lit hearth, convey, I believe, the image of a writer dedicated to his craft. I've also included an autographed copy for you to hang in your office.

Please understand this letter is written in the spirit of genuine concern for you as the respected editor of an esteemed literary journal. The last thing I'd want is for you to experience the kind of debilitating regret that comes from accidentally rejecting a world-renowned writer like myself.

I look forward to receiving your acceptance letter in the following days.

Sincerely,
Kevin Herbst

The Crossing

House prices plummeting. Commercial and residential building at a thirty-year low. Historic unemployment. All bad news I seemed to find every morning in the *Arizona Republic* business section, and, taking it all in, I'd experience that same queasiness and morbid curiosity I felt when rolling past a car accident on the I-10. All that twisted metal and smashed glass, the white sheet flecked with blood. Nothing good comes from looking. Nothing good comes from dwelling on gloom. But I'd scan the headlines anyway for some indication of economic upturn and find nothing, no hope on the horizon, a mess and getting worse, and foolishly I'd read on and chew my Frosted Shredded Wheats and fight back a nervous flutter in my lower guts when I fixed on something particularly disquieting.

Yet, I smiled. I ate with vigor and even listened with interest as my wife, Kendra, thumbed through *Genteel Baby* and went on about something she thought our unborn Joey couldn't live without, a Native American infant carrier or a diaper bag with solar panels.

Though if she'd looked closely, she'd have seen a damp spot on the newspaper where my hand had rested. Kendra doesn't read the business section, and only the most superficial details of my work enter our conversations: high-profile clients, office drama, what brand of handbag the secretaries use, their nail and hair color. The truth: business was bad, the worst it'd been since I depleted our savings four years ago to buy the firm. I never told Kendra that business was bad. She has a fear of poverty, a childhood insecurity I've tried to understand. She can get weepy about her childhood of hand-me-down shoes and day-old bread stores and bland breakfasts of multigrain cereals cooked for hours in a crockpot. Then when she was ten, the winds of fortune changed. My father-in-law bought a bankrupt bottling company. He started a tropical fruit juice line. He became a millionaire overnight. The family bought a mansion on Lake of the Isles in Minneapolis. Kendra drove a Mercedes to high school. She had the bridge of her nose surgically smoothed. She hated the hand-to-mouth existence of her lower middle class childhood. I get it. She wants a better life for Joey. She doesn't want a failed, penniless husband. I get that, too.

I should mention that I own an architecture firm in Phoenix—four architects, two secretaries, two interns from Arizona State, a receptionist, and an outrageous lease on the third floor of a very modern glass and steel building that overlooks part of the Biltmore golf course. In the gravy days, we had so much business we were turning it away. Everyone was building and remodeling then, lured in by the easy credit, and suddenly, almost overnight, the boom was over. Banks failed. Credit dried up. Now you look out from Route 60 and see the half-finished wooden skeletons of homes browning in the desert sun. Like everyone else, I started hoarding pennies.

I dimmed the office lights, set the thermostat to 81, swapped out the incandescent light bulbs for the compact fluorescent kind, and did away with the glut of free snacks and highly caffeinated beverages in the breakroom refrigerator. And when my accountant told me to trim more or lay somebody off, I cancelled our cleaning service, EarthMaids, these hippie women who drive white Priuses and tout their environmentally safe products that, frankly, reek of vinegar and grapefruit. They'd leave sermonizing notes on my computer keyboard if they found even one empty Coke can in the trash. And they weren't cheap.

I could clean things up myself, at least until work picked up. How hard could it be? Not that I told my employees. I didn't want panic or rumor. It doesn't really inspire confidence to see your boss in yellow rubber gloves spritzing up the bathroom mirrors. So I stayed late, scrubbed urinals and toilets, emptied the trash and vacuumed floors. I'll admit the quality of the work was subpar. Usually I was exhausted and in a rush to get home. Katrina, one of my interns, complained. "Look at the dust on these lampshades," she said. "Have you seen the smudges on the bathroom mirror? There's no soap in the dispensers. Sloppy." I didn't know lampshades needed dusting.

I lasted two weeks. I didn't have time. I'm a busy man, a business owner, an architect. I considered asking my interns to clean, considered lecturing them on the value of hard work and on taking pride in one's workplace, and then hinting at the performance evaluation I'd soon write for them. There was Katrina, a platinum blonde architecture major from Scottsdale with skin meticulously tanned the color of a saddle and lips the size of garden slugs. She favored denim miniskirts and UGG boots and long acrylic nails painted a lurid red. I doubted she'd ever touched a toilet brush or pushed a vacuum across a floor. And there was Matt, a chiseled frat boy, a former high school football star from Flagstaff, who spent most of the day appraising, not very subtly, the curve and sway of Katrina's butt. They'd refuse. I was sure. There'd be mutiny.

Over lunch with a friend at the Grand Orange, I complained about the plight of the small business owner in this fragile economy. Stewart and I were fraternity brothers at ASU. He was a podiatrist with a growing practice off 24th Street. I wanted commiseration, I wanted to hear things would get better. I mentioned—I don't know why, perhaps for nothing more than sympathy—that I'd just let my cleaning service go and was now doing their work at nights. Stewart said nothing, only shot me a grave look and then scratched a phone number on his napkin.

"God, you're not a janitor," he said, as he pushed the napkin across the table. "There's this woman and her son. Yolanda's her name. Mexicans. Thirteen an hour for both of them, damn good workers, always on time, and they never say anything, just nose to the grindstone. You almost forget they're there."

I stared at the number. "Mexicans. Mexicans from Mexico?" I imagined the sad, oily faces of day laborers eyeing me like homeless puppies every time I pulled into Home Depot, the desperate gaze of pie-faced women selling tamales in the Safeway parking lot. I was skeptical. I thought of stolen office equipment, long-distance phone calls to remote Mexican villages, a dark-skinned pigmy sleeping in the storage closet and bathing in the bathroom sink. "Is it safe?" I asked.

Stewart waved his hand dismissively. "It's not like they're real employees. You don't like them, you fire them, you call Immigration." He belched into his hand. "There won't be a problem, trust me. These people aim to please. You got their purse strings in your hot little hands."

Thirteen an hour. I followed the mechanical up-and-down of Stewart's jaw as it obliterated a slice of French bread. Thirteen an hour, a bargain, a fraction of what the hippie cleaners charged. I sniffed the tips of my red, raw fingers. They smelled like Pine-Sol.

That afternoon, I called Yolanda. Our short conversation reached the very limits of my high school Spanish. Work, sweep, windows, trash. We understood each other perfectly, and more important: *Trece dolares por hora.* I wanted that to be clear. We made arrangements: she and her son Hector would clean twice a week, Monday and Wednesday mornings. "No clean at night?" Yolanda asked. "No," I said without explanation. "*Hay algun problema?*" Of course there wasn't a problem.

So that was the deal. A service rendered. A fee paid. And like a good employer, I opened my wallet on Wednesday and handed over the cash. No hassle of federal withholding, no state tax, no Medicare or social security deductions. Just cash and a thank you.

They were efficient, thorough, and unobtrusive. And Stewart was right, I hardly noticed them. When Yolanda emptied my trash or if I passed her in the hallway, she had the uncanny ability to minimize herself, to avoid attention, and when I did say something, a cheery *Buenos días* or *Cómo estás* she stared at the floor and smiled bashfully. Hector also had that diminutive quality, but less so. He walked around the office in gray Dickies and a sleeveless undershirt that showed off the swell of his biceps and the chiseled lineaments of his forearms, backbone ramrod straight, head thrown back, a pair of oil-black sunglasses fused to his face. Tattooed in red on his left bicep was a phoenix with outstretched, translucent wings and a menacing gaze. In its sharp talons, the bird held the number 602. Admittedly, the tattoo and baggy clothes and shaved head gave me pause. Gang affiliation? Was he dangerous? Maybe there'd been some bad decisions in his past. Chalk it up to youth and inexperience. Maybe he'd seen the error of his ways and now wanted to make an honest living. That's what I imagined for Hector. He scrubbed urinals and toilets, pushed a vacuum across the floors. How dangerous could he be? In my mind bad characters didn't clean offices. They robbed them. And I was the guy offering opportunity and success, the benevolent human looking past the sleek machismo and silly tattoo, into the heart. That's what I imagined for myself. But that didn't stop me from circulating a vague interoffice electronic memo on the importance of securing valuables and other personal items in the workplace.

Katrina complained. She'd tiptoed into my office on Hector and Yolanda's first day, clutching her brown Gucci purse to her chest. "That kid—" She smacked her gum loudly, a small annoyance I'd been meaning to talk to her about. I cut her off.

"What kid?" I reclined my chair and stared up at her. "You mean Hector? He does have a name. You have a concern about him?"

She leaned over my desk, practically whispering, her blue eyes wide and panicked: "Whatever. That Mexican kid. He looks like"—her eyes moved over the wall behind me—"he looks like a criminal." She intensified her grip on the purse, practically shoving it into her ample, bronzed cleavage. "What happened to those other people, those women?"

A vacuum cleaner hummed in the hallway.

I was preachy. I'll admit it. I was condescending. I spoke slowly. "Weren't you complaining last week about the smudged windows and the empty soap dispensers?"

"I didn't mean fire them," Katrina said.

"Does it really matter who cleans the office?" I rubbed my palms together and contemplated the perfect crescent of Katrina's eyebrows, her fried platinum hair and enormous pouty lips. I felt giddy, like a man who'd stretched a dollar. I felt generous and world-wise.

"Does it matter what these people look like?" I said. "Where they come from? Not all of us have the same opportunities in life, Katrina. Or maybe you wouldn't mind cleaning up?"

She turned and ran from my office.

As the months passed, I had no complaints. Hector and Yolanda worked quickly. No dilly-dallying. They sweated as they worked—that impressed me. I could see the shiny drops beading on their foreheads and upper lips. They were a bargain, a find, a hundred times better than the hippie cleaners. No sermonizing notes, and I was saving a small fortune.

Then one Monday I got into work a little later than usual, completely drained from having passed half the night enduring Kendra's wall-rattling snores—a bummer of late pregnancy no one warned me about—and the other half batting away our smelly, geriatric tabby, Buttons, from the Lazyboy where I was curled up in a thin blanket. A man stopped me outside the building lobby. He was thick around the chest, thick arms and thighs, the build of a professional wrestler, with a pale, doggish face and a shaved head ravaged by the Phoenix sun. "Mr. Fenton," he said in a hoarse voice, much higher than I'd expected. "David Fenton, the architect, right?"

My hand rested on the door handle. I was rushing. We had a twelve o'clock deadline on a condo remodel in Scottsdale. There were still some details to hash out. "I'm in a bit of a rush," I said.

I thought he might be a contractor drumming up some business, but he seemed too put-together, too clean and manicured. I caught a whiff of his cologne, sharp and musky and cheap like something my father might have splashed on in his prime. There was something overly affected about him that brought to mind the tough guy, the vigilante, the good, misunderstood protagonist of at least a dozen TV shows. He wore a black leather jacket with the collar raised, though the heat was already pushing ninety, and a starched white T-shirt tucked into grayish stonewashed jeans. And then it hit me: he's a cop. And as if reading my mind, he pulled out a Maricopa County Sheriff badge and waved it in my face. "Detective Sherman," he said. "I only need a second."

My mind whirled. Had somebody died? Had there been a break-in? A stolen car? Were they investigating a client? Or me? I never thought of Yolanda and Hector. I waited. Sherman said nothing, just looked me up and down, a wry smile I couldn't interpret creasing his thin, freckled lips. He pulled a pair of dark sunglasses from his jacket pocket, breathed on the mirrored lenses and polished them on his shirt. "Got an appointment?" he asked. "Gonna turn over some money?" His head swiveled on his thick neck, his gaze taking in the building, the sway of the palm trees, the manicured hibiscus lining the parking lot, as if he had all the time in the world. "A lot of people turning over money in these parts. Making money and not caring about anyone else." He smiled, showing a row of small white teeth.

I didn't follow, and I didn't like his preachy tone. A feeling of annoyance slid in behind the anxiety of a moment ago. I felt Sherman was toying with me, for what reason I didn't know, wielding his badge, wasting my time. "Is there something I can do for you, Detective?" I said it curtly, to convey my annoyance.

"That's right," Sherman said. "You're a busy man. I just need you to do something for me." He stepped toward the curb. "Could you look up at the building?" he asked. I did, not knowing what I was looking for. Lights were on. Silhouettes danced behind the shaded glass. "And that building across the street," Sherman said.

I couldn't hide my irritation. "And what am I looking for?"

"My sister owns a cleaning service," he said. "They used to clean a lot of these offices. Cleaned your office, in fact."

A drop of sweat trickled down my back. The sun clawed at my neck. I suddenly knew where this was going.

"And then about three months ago," he said, "her clients started letting her go. She took it personally, Mr. Fenton. She works hard, her employees work hard. She's honest, bends over backwards for some of these pampered snobs, and they dismissed her, without explanation. Do you know why? Illegals, Mr. Fenton. Wetbacks, border bandits, fence fairies, whatever you want to call them. They come here to take our jobs. They don't learn our language. They steal right off our plates. And you know who opens the door and lets them get comfortable? People like you, Mr. Fenton."

My mouth had gone dry.

At that moment, Hector and Yolanda pulled into the parking lot in a sputtering, red Chevy Cavalier, found a space not far from where Sherman and I stood, and started unloading the car, pulling out buckets, rags, a vacuum, and a mop. As they walked toward the building, Sherman and I watched. Yolanda smiled. "Good morning," she said in an accent so thick it sounded like each word had a sharp edge.

I looked away, I stared at the concrete curbing around the lawn, I said nothing.

Sherman jumped to attention, clicked the heels of his thick black boots and pulled the door open. "*Buenos días*," he said, in a high voice without a trace of gringo accent. "*Cómo están?*" He made a deep, courtly bow as they passed. Yolanda's face turned a deep red. She leaned forward and rounded her shoulders. Hector stared at the ground, his black shades reflecting the travertine tile in the lobby.

Sherman watched their quick progress to the elevator. "Yolanda and Hector Molina," he said. "And I have a feeling that in about two minutes I'd find them wiping piss off your toilet seats. Right?"

I opened my mouth. One guttural syllable belched out and then nothing else. I was angry, scared, conflicted. I wanted to tell Sherman exactly what I thought of him and where to go, tell him to speak with my lawyer (if I could afford one). I wanted to smile, shake my head and grin dumbly, tell him I'd made a mistake we could rectify without any long, drawn-out legal process.

"I could suspend your business license," Sherman said in barely more than a whisper, as if the phrase itself were an obscenity. "I could storm this place with ten officers to bring them in. It'd be something. The newspapers love those stories. I could shut you down—for a while at least, long enough to make it hurt." A black mist hovered on the edges of my vision. I wanted to sit down. "But I'll tell you what I'll do. . . ." Sherman stopped. His features—the squint of his eyes, the hard set of his jaw—softened. He looked up at the sky and sighed. I suddenly felt the ground solidifying under my feet, felt my lungs open up and catch a full breath of air.

"They're like parasites, Mr. Fenton. Don't you see that? They'll feed until there's nothing left. They're mongrels." Sherman put his sunglasses on. My expectant, eager-to-please face bobbed in their chrome reflection. "Wednesday morning, 9:30, I'll be back for them. If they're not here, I'll assume a little bird whispered in their ear. If that happens, I'll do something about that ungrateful bird. You understand, Mr. Fenton?" I nodded. Sherman turned away and then stopped. "Hey, you should call my sister. She'll make you a good deal, Mr. Fenton. I'll tell her to expect your call."

When I got up to my office, I called a lawyer, this guy named Bereski I'd been paired with about a month ago on the Biltmore's back nine. He'd given me his card.

He didn't say anything until I finished, just made little puffing noises into the phone as I narrated the events of the past few months, gasped when I told him about Sherman, as if he were the devil himself. I wanted to know if Sherman could shut me down.

"These new laws are clear," Bereski said. "A company that knowingly hires a worker who's in the country illegally will have its license suspended. But this business with his sister"—Bereski's voice pitched higher, vibrated with loyal outrage—"this is coercion, a threat, a conflict of interest, a violation of your rights. It impugns his case. We can fight this." Bereski cleared his throat. "And let me say that in this trying economic climate"—I thought I heard fingers punching at a calculator—"you'll find our rates affordable. We understand the challenges of the small business owner."

A vacuum hummed down the hall. Grit rattled through its plastic tubes. Cleaner hissed from spray bottles. Plastic trash liners deployed. In the parking lot below, a weed eater buzzed, and then a voice called out, "*No tenemos tiempo.*" I didn't say anything.

"Mr. Fenton," Bereski said. "Mr. Fenton, are you there?"

I reclined my chair. "Or he can just take them and it'll be over."

"Yes," Bereski said, all the outrage gone out of his voice. "That's also an option."

I told him I'd get back to him.

I sat at my desk and stared at a blueprint, trying to lose myself in work. Lines and numbers floated across the page, danced, came in and out of focus.

Someone knocked at the door. Yolanda peeked in. "I sorry," she said. She looked at the floor. "Trash. Clean windows." I stood, yes, stood and waved her in, smiling graciously. She went about her work. I couldn't help thinking that I'd never really looked at her until that moment. She had her hair in a braided ponytail, wore bleach-spotted jeans and a maroon T-shirt with a stretched neck. She wasn't unattractive, the ample swell of her breasts against the shirt, the curve of strong legs in those tight jeans, full lips. Her face and hands were a little freckled. Maybe she'd worked outdoors at one time, picking fruit or something. She was still pretty and, I realized, not much older than I.

What did she want in life? Where did she live? I knew nothing about her. I'd driven past Phoenix's tenements, the crumbling cinder block and cracked windows. I'd seen the disheveled children with sticky mouths and hands, men peering out from stairwells, the parking lots of afflicted, immobile cars, places accustomed to the drone of helicopters and the blare of sirens. Did she live there? And where had she come from?

Two years ago Kendra and I spent a week in Mazatlan, drinking margaritas in the looming shadows of colonial churches and attentively browning our skin on the beaches, venturing into the local market to haggle over the price of leather purses and vanilla. It all seemed so quaint, the smiling, unhurried natives, the pealing church bells, the mariachi music trilling in the background as if it were the soundtrack of their simple lives. Is that where she came from? I wanted to believe it was.

When I got home that evening, I was exhausted. I didn't want to talk. I wanted alcohol. I wanted to chew food and flip through channels until I fell into a stupor.

But Kendra was energized, practically glowing. She wanted to tell me every detail of her day. She'd been nesting: vacuuming floors, assembling things, sanitizing bottles and pacifiers. She was breathing heavily, and the hair around her forehead was dark with sweat. "Do you like the bedding I ordered?" she asked. We stood in the nursery looking at the crib.

I picked up a small pillow with a pattern of grinning brown monkeys swinging from trees. "Nice," I said. I took in the room, each stick of furniture, each soft, sanitized surface. The Birchwood crib and changing table came from a Pennsylvania company that specialized in Amish furnishings. In the garage there was a stroller that looked like NASA engineers had designed it. We had a breast pump on order that cost more than my first car. And then there were the tiny pants and shirts hanging in the closet from Scottsdale boutiques with names like Jacadi Paris and Dapper Child. I couldn't help seeing a trail of receipts extending into the future, for more clothes, preschool, swim lessons, summer camp, proms, and college tuition.

Kendra hovered protectively above the crib. She took the pillow from me and rearranged it with the others, then ran her hand over the quilted blanket. "It's organic cotton, twice as much, but you don't get all those pesticides. You know, they never wash out. Could you imagine little Joey breathing that in?"

I lifted a diaper from the changing table. It was no bigger than a washcloth. "No," I said, "terrible," though I couldn't remember what she'd asked. A lawn mower had fired up across the street, and over the whir of the engine I heard rushed voices speaking Spanish. I looked through the open blinds at the two men attending to my neighbor's yard, skin like caramel, upper lips with the faintest suggestion of a mustache. One jogged behind the mower and the other raked furiously at a patch of decorative rock. It was like they were racing, as if someone with a stopwatch were overseeing their work from behind the oleander.

I thought of Mrs. Lufkin, our neighbor. She'd lived in the beige Craftsman two doors down for the last fifty years, a big-boned Jewish woman who had fled Germany after *Kristallnacht*. She often brought us apple strudel and big copper pots of matzo soup. "You're too thin," she'd tell Kendra, pinching her cheeks. "We need to fatten you up." She wagged her finger if she saw us wearing short sleeves in February. She was gone now, had moved away six months ago to a retirement community in Sun City. She left after two men broke into her house.

There'd been a string of burglaries in the neighborhood. We spoke with the Phoenix Police Department. They assigned more officers to our area. We formed a neighborhood watch. We hired a retired Mesa cop to drive the streets at night.

It was about three in the morning when Mrs. Lufkin heard voices, she told us later. She got out of bed to investigate and found two men in the dining room stuffing her wedding silver into a pillowcase. She reached for the phone, but one of the men wrenched it from her and threw it against the wall. They didn't say anything, just pushed her aside and continued rummaging through the house for another five minutes, then jumped the back fence into the alleyway and drove off.

Kendra and I saw the police cruiser's blue and red lights slashing across our bedroom walls. We went over and found Mrs. Lufkin sitting on her couch, a crumpled, ashen figure wrapped in a purple bathrobe. A Phoenix police officer, a short, balding man with crumbs on the collar of his black uniform, inspected the living room.

"Can you give me a description of the men?" he asked, a pen poised above a clipboard. He looked as if he'd just woken up.

"They were"—Mrs. Lufkin's voice quivered. She looked at me. She looked at Kendra. Her spotted hands shook. I knew what she'd say before she said it. Kendra knew. The fat police officer knew—"Mexicans." And the way she said it, drawing out the first syllable, made the word sound like a slur. "Dirty Mexicans who smelled like beans and sweat."

Kendra stood there with one hand covering her mouth and the other resting on that small bump just under her belly button. I put my arm around her. She stared silently at the wall as if the whole terrifying scene were playing out again: Mrs. Lufkin watching as these men rifled through her drawers and closets. But I knew it wasn't Mrs. Lufkin she saw. She saw herself.

In bed later, Kendra tossed and turned, tugged at the duvet, held her breath when a car passed. She sat up suddenly. "What if they come here?" she said.

"They won't." I was tired, not in the mood at that moment to ease her fears. "It's not worth losing sleep over. They're gone."

She started to cry. "You can't protect us. No one can. They're everywhere."

I reached out to hold her, but she slapped my hand.

"Don't you see? These people want what we have and they don't care how they get it." She turned and sobbed into the pillow.

The next morning she wouldn't speak to me. She didn't look up from her cereal when I left for work.

That afternoon she called the office.

"You have to come home." Her voice was a whisper. I thought I hadn't understood her. She panted into the phone. Then hung up. I called back. She didn't answer.

I swore into the phone as it rang and rang and then went to voicemail. I didn't have time for this. I had a lunch meeting with an attorney looking to build a new office off Cactus Road. A big project.

We needed it badly. But what if something had happened? I couldn't help thinking that. Kendra. Mrs. Lufkin. Maybe the baby. I told my secretary to cancel lunch.

Kendra was sitting on the couch when I got home. She stared at the closed plantation shutters, biting at her lower lip. She looked ready to cry.

I stood above her, breathless.

"I don't want him here." She pointed at the shutters.

I was confused. A hedge trimmer buzzed in the front yard. A rake scratched the sidewalk. I lifted the shutters and saw our gardener, Frank, and his helper cutting back the yellow hibiscus that edged the yard. They'd come every week for the past two years. "What? Is it Frank?" I said.

"It's not Frank," Kendra said. Her eyes were glassy, her face expressionless. "It's that man who comes with him. That Mexican."

I sank into a chair and pressed with my fingertips at a dull pain between my eyes. A feeling of helplessness came over me. I knew I wouldn't be designing a law office off Cactus Road. I knew my firm would feel it. Maybe I'd have to let someone go. Who would it be? And looking at Kendra, at the irrational fear in her eyes, I knew there was nothing I could do to calm her, nothing I could say to restore safety. She'd wanted to live in historic Phoenix, wanted the antique charm of a whitewashed home older than our grandparents, the carefully manicured yard and sprawling porch. What did she expect? This is what happens in a city, I wanted to tell her. This is urban living. This is the price you pay.

I gripped the armrests. "Fine, I'll tell Frank."

And then for two days she moped around the house. She barely slept. She didn't get dressed in the morning. She called me at least three times a day to tell me about some suspicious person passing on the street or how she thought we should move to North Scottsdale or Ahwatuckee.

But when I got home on the third day, she'd actually showered and gotten dressed. The shutters were open, the table set with china and wineglasses. The aroma of cooked meat filled the house.

Kendra stood over the table in a yellow sundress.

"Wow," I said. "What's the deal?"

She didn't say anything, just came up to me with this shy, lopsided smile and kissed me. Her tongue tasted like mint. "Look at this," she said, lifting the local section of the *Arizona Republic* from the coffee table and pointing to a headline circled in red.

"Anonymous Tip Helps Police Catch Willo Thieves," I read.

Kendra touched the hem of her dress. "The men who broke into Mrs. Lufkin's house. The police got them in some kind of raid. Illegals. A network of them. The police have their fingerprints. People saw their faces. They can identify them. Thank God." Her right hand rested on her stomach.

That was six months ago. We hadn't spoken of Mrs. Lufkin or the burglars since.

I closed the blinds so Kendra wouldn't see out the nursery window. She rubbed my neck. "Long day?" she asked.

I already knew I wouldn't tell her about Sherman, not a word about Yolanda and Hector. What was the point? She'd pace the floor and lecture me if I did. She'd bring up Mrs. Lufkin. She wouldn't sleep that night or the next. Give them up. That's what she'd say, without equivocation. She was right. There was family. There was a baby coming, a mortgage, food to put on the table, bills to pay. Really, who were Hector and Yolanda to me? They weren't family, they weren't friends. They really weren't even my employees.

I closed my eyes. Kendra's small hands moved over my shoulders. I tried to imagine Wednesday. The snap of handcuffs, mug shots and fingerprinting. And then what? Deportation? I wanted to believe Yolanda and Hector would begin the journey back to their ancestral village, back to the charm of the small hamlet I'd imagined for them, the mariachi music and the molasses pace of a provincial life. I believed it, I hoped it, and that image seemed to obscure some nagging questions I couldn't answer as I'd watched Yolanda empty my trash can that morning. Why had she crossed that border? Why had she come here?

Sherman came early.

I'd thought about staying home—a headache, allergies, sour stomach, leprosy, anything not to see Sherman's vigilante production. When my employees told me what happened, I could feign surprise, shake my head and decry the System. A real tragedy. We could have a moment of silence, take up a collection to support a

Nicaraguan orphan. But I had to go. I feared Sherman, feared he'd wield his badge and harass my employees. There was Margarita, our receptionist, who in the right light bore a striking resemblance to Salma Hayek, and Ricardo, one of my architects. Both were born in the States, as American as Miley Cyrus and Jimmy Stewart.

I was at my desk when I heard the front door open. Heavy shoes beat across the carpet. A chair struck the floor. Silence. And then a sad, piercing scream. I was on my feet, moving toward the lobby. Doors opened and heads peered into the hallway. I told everyone to stay in their offices. Margarita passed me with a horrified look on her face and disappeared into the break room.

Hector and I got to the lobby at the same time.

Yolanda sat on the carpet, rocking back and forth and wailing, legs crumpled beneath her, hands cuffed behind her back. Long strings of black hair stuck to her wet face. Sherman, in a black flak vest with *Maricopa County Sheriff* embroidered across the chest in thick yellow lettering, stood above her, face flushed, hand resting on the gun at his hip. A faint grin pulled at his thin lips. He looked up at Hector.

"*Ven aquí*," he said, raising a thick, dry finger and shaking it at Hector. "On your knees. You hear me, motherfucker?"

Hector stood there, arms rigid at his side. He stared at his mother.

"Down," Sherman repeated, this time with a tinny growl that came off as more effeminate than forceful. I watched Hector, the rise and fall of his chest, the slight bend in his knees. He looked at Sherman and then at me, a look of complete understanding. The System, privilege, the haves and the have-nots, the trap we'd set for him and Yolanda—he knew everything.

And then, just as I thought Hector would go quietly and I could go back to my office and forget all this unpleasantness, Yolanda shouted something. I jumped. Sherman flinched. It sounded like a war cry. I didn't recognize her. This wasn't the face of the meek woman who dusted lampshades and wiped countertops, but the face of a woman ripe with anger. And then I understood. She was telling Hector to run.

Hector dropped his arms. His head twisted on his shoulders. His eyes locked onto the door at the end of the hallway, an emergency exit that led to a dimly lit stairwell and down to the parking lot. He then fixed on me, the only obstacle to his retreat, the man in cahoots with the guy who'd just cuffed his mom and thrown her to the floor. He came at me, breathing heavily, baring a row of perfect white teeth framed between full lips. I felt his hands gripped firmly around my neck, nails cutting into the soft flesh at my hairline, palms compressing my windpipe. His enraged face came to life in front of mine like an enormous parade balloon. "I'll kill you," he hissed in my ear. Then I was down on the carpet, shielding my head. Sherman lumbered past, his thick boots beating a slow, heavy rhythm on the floor. But Hector was already gone.

Sherman canvassed the parking lot, poked around in the dark crevices of the juniper and hibiscus, called in three officers to scour the golf course and the high-end strip mall up the street. Nothing.

"So what are you going to do?" I demanded of Sherman. My voice shook. I couldn't seem to catch my breath.

Sherman stood with one foot propped up on the bumper of his white Crown Victoria, carefully picking grass stubble from his pants. His black flak vest was stained white with salt that had leached through under the arms and up the back. His bald, sun-battered scalp was the color of boiled hotdogs.

He didn't look up. "About what?" he said, clucking his tongue at a stubborn cocklebur in the lining of his sock. Yolanda sat in the back of the car, head bent forward, a sad form behind the tinted windows.

My fingers traced the red, inflamed lines on my neck. I didn't know how I'd explain them to Kendra. "Didn't you hear him? He said he'd kill me. That's a threat. What are you—" I stopped. Sherman shook his head, threw me a what-do-I-care look.

"Didn't think about that when you hired them. You just wanted to save a buck. Maybe now you're beginning to see. It's war out there. Every day I tell my little daughter that."

"And what about Yolanda?"

"Who cares?" Sherman flicked his sunglasses open and put them on. "Back to Mexico. One less problem. One less drain on the system. You should be happy. All of us should be happy." He opened the car door and slid in. "I have to write a report today. Haven't decided yet what I'll say. I might feel generous. Or maybe not." He ran his thumb under his nose. "I spoke with my sister last night. She says you haven't called."

Sherman slammed the car door and accelerated through the

parking lot, pulled onto Camelback and was gone. Yolanda never looked back.

Hector's faced loomed in my mind, took root there. I imagined him crouching in the darkness, seething, biding his time. Or maybe he'd send someone, a henchman from the gang. I saw him in the dark-skinned men mowing lawns or moving heavy furniture, the men pushing ice cream carts down the streets or driving through back alleys to pick through our garbage. The raw, red lines on my neck burned—in the sun, in the shower, under the slight graze of my collar. (I told Kendra, without much explanation, that I'd tripped and fallen backwards into a hibiscus bush. She laughed. "Clumsy you," she said, and kissed my forehead.)

Work continued. My employees talked about other things.

EarthMaids, with their scented organic products and moralizing notes, were again under my employ. Every time I looked at them, I thought I saw a smirk on their pale faces, as if they knew well the power that had brought them back to me.

Two weeks passed. We got a small project for a set of condos in south Scottsdale. We had a deadline. My neck was healing. I'd almost forgotten Hector.

Then I saw him again, pacing the turn lane in the middle of Thomas Road, waiting for a break in the long line of cars moving toward Central Avenue. I thought he was a mirage, the baggy gray Dickies and long white T-shirt, the shaved head and that silly bird tattooed on his bicep. I blinked quickly. I kept waiting for his face to morph into someone else's, someone I didn't know and would never meet. I felt panic. He wasn't far from our house. Kendra was there.

The traffic moved forward and then stalled. Hector came toward me. I locked the car doors, leaned forward and grabbed the steering wheel. He kept walking, didn't look down, crossed two lanes of traffic at a quick jog and then disappeared into the crowd at the bus stop.

I called Kendra. She didn't answer. I tried again. Nothing.

The light changed. I worked through the gears, weaved like a maniac around cars, turned onto our street with tires screaming. I pulled into the driveway and ran for the door, pushed it open and listened. I heard the reassuring hiss of water from a faucet, a cabinet opening, the clink of small glass containers—makeup remover, face soap, pimple cream. The bathroom door opened and a swath of buttery light colored the hallway.

Kendra stood there, a silhouette with an enormous belly. "How was work?" she asked.

I laughed nervously. My fingers shook as they worked the deadbolt. "Fine," I said. And then: "You off to bed?"

"I'm exhausted." She spoke with a breathy whisper, as if she were already tucked in for the night.

"I'm not far behind," I said, pulling at my tie. I felt I'd overreacted, felt the figure with the expressionless face crossing Thomas Road had been a coincidence, or maybe an apparition, or maybe someone else, a tattooed gangbanger with sagging pants, like a thousand others wandering Phoenix.

Then Kendra, the handle of the bedroom door twisting in her small, delicate hand, said something that stopped me cold:

"There's a manila envelope on your desk. It was strange. Somebody left it on the porch this afternoon, rang the bell, and when I opened the door, no one. It has your name on it. Something for work?"

I felt as if a cold hand had brushed the tiny hairs on my neck.

"Probably." I tried to sound unconcerned, but a rushing sound filled my ears.

Kendra sighed. She'd already lost interest, was already half-asleep. "Good night," she said.

I listened to her naked feet pad across the wooden floor, heard the fluffing of pillows, the rustle of sheets. And then nothing. I stood there in the darkness and took in the streetlamp's yellow light streaming through the plantation shutters.

I knew.

He'd walked the flagstone path to the porch, stood at my door, maybe peered into the picture window and seen Kendra there, painting her nails, gluing pieces of colored paper into a scrapbook, weeping with Oprah.

Kendra's yucca and parlor palm threw strange shadows across the walls. The evaporative cooler kicked on. Air rattled through the vent, and for a moment I thought I heard two low voices somewhere deep within the ducts.

I went to the kitchen and poured Hennessy over a knot of ice, drank, and then drank again. Ten minutes later, somewhat recuperated, I was at my desk turning over the manila envelope. I opened it, reached in and pulled out a stack of blank letterhead. *Fenton Architecture, David Fenton.* My right leg jerked, toppling the wicker garbage basket under my desk. My letterhead.

I quickly thumbed through the stack. Hector had written on the last sheet, something in black permanent marker, sharp, angry writing not unlike the graffiti that blighted the walls and billboards downtown. The marker's odor burned my eyes. I squinted, trying to make out the words. *Soy una voz que grita nel desierto.* I spoke the words out loud. Their meaning came to me suddenly. *I am a voice that cries in the desert.* The words knocked the breath out of me. Was this a joke lost in translation, a veiled threat, the coded, brass-knuckled language of the streets?

Was it time to panic? Was it time to gather my fragile world into itself, to build a wall and dig in? I'd always leaned toward pacifism, had preferred from an early age to fight my battles in the classroom and now, as an adult, to beat the competition by winning more contracts and turning over more money than they did. As far as I was concerned, physical altercations were a non-issue in my circle, an inner-city phenomenon or a third world problem about which Kendra and I would shake our heads and mumble things like "horrible!" and "disgraceful!" and "poor darlings!" as we munched popcorn and stared at news footage of fat dictators waving to cheering crowds or eight-year-old kids in Zimbabwe with AK-47s. But now after all this, his coming to my home, the envelope, none of that seemed so distant. The war had come closer. Or maybe it was here.

I'd never been in a fight. I was a courteous driver, slow to anger when confronted with stupidity, patient when faced with daunting lines and subpar customer service. I avoided talking politics and religion in the office, and played sports with no physical contact, favoring a long fairway and the leather grip of my Callaway driver or the crack of serves and the dry shuffle of rubber on clay. I wasn't prepared for any of this. I didn't know how to make it stop.

I thought of Kendra asleep in the next room, of our unborn child. I thought of Mrs. Lufkin. I thought of Hector. What is *he* capable of? I didn't know, and that terrified me.

I didn't sleep. I had no appetite. I couldn't shut off my imagination, couldn't help spinning out macabre scenarios: my desk and office walls splashed with blood, an iron grip around my throat, a knife jammed between my ribs. I called Sherman and left a message. He never called back.

Work picked up. We were having a baby. I'd almost forgotten.

Kendra bought a nightgown for the hospital, a purple low-cut silk thing. The sight of it aroused me. She complained of Braxton Hicks. She snored viciously at night, a rasping exhalation like the flatulent discharge from a whoopee cushion. I slept on the couch with Buttons, breathing in her rank geriatric stench all night. Hector's enraged face, larger than life weeks ago, began to diminish into a distant uneasiness. I assumed he'd forgotten about me.

Then the day before Joey was born, I was working late, clearing my desk for the two weeks I'd planned to take off. I'd just locked up the office and was walking to my car when I heard something: the scrape of shoes on asphalt, the brush of pant legs. I turned and saw a man approaching me, a stooped figure, shoulders rounded, pants ragged at the knees, a white T-shirt smeared with grime. A panhandler. A bum looking for a handout. He came closer, stepping into the streetlamp's yellow light. And then I saw the face, strangely familiar but beaten out of shape, the left eye swollen shut and leaking a clear fluid, the upper lip bloody, an open gash on the left cheek yellow with infection. I barely recognized him without the black sunglasses. Hector.

My heart accelerated. I gripped my keys like a weapon, lifted my briefcase as if it were a shield. I thought of jumping the cinder block fence surrounding the parking lot, running down Camelback and screaming for help. But there was no need for that. Hector limped toward me. His left arm, blotched with bruises, hung lifeless at his side, and with his right arm he held a place just under his ribs. Breath rasping in his throat, he sat down heavily on a parking barrier. When he looked up at me, his good eye took me in at a glance, the linen slacks and Italian loafers, the calfskin briefcase in my right hand.

"You never paid us for Monday." Hector stared at his scuffed black Converses. The fire had gone out of him, the fight was gone.

I thought he might pass out right there on the asphalt. "Pay me and I'll leave," he said. "You'll never see me again. You'll never hear from me."

I looked at him, at the stiff bristle of dark fuzz on his head, at the festering sore on his cheek. He couldn't touch me. He couldn't even lift his arms. I knew he was desperate, emptied of all the shaded, muscled machismo he'd strutted around the office two weeks ago. Why else would he have ventured back here to collect a few dollars he knew I probably wouldn't give him? I could've made a call. The police would have arrived in minutes. He wouldn't get far. And why should I pay him? I touched the back of my neck. My fingers grazed the scabbed marks there. He'd laid hands on me, threatened me, come to my home, terrorized me with his cryptic message. But then knowing I'd never see him again, near my house, at my work, dispelled my resentment. I wanted to dissolve whatever connection he thought we had, and if it cost a few bucks, fine. I wanted to sleep through the night again, sleep deeply and soundly without a shadow clouding my thoughts. I pulled a hundred dollars from my wallet. Hector's hand trembled as he took the money. His knuckles were raw and bleeding.

"That's twice what I pay you. You understand?" Despite everything, I felt charitable. I was ready to forgive. I wanted him to see that. But he didn't look at the money, didn't thank me, just stared at those black Converses as he pushed the bills into the front pocket of his billowing pants. A helicopter passed overhead. A thick shaft of light vented from its belly. We watched it move over the building and continue west. Hector didn't say anything. He didn't move.

"So what happened to you?" I asked.

"Why the fuck do you care?" Hector said fiercely. And then: "What do you think happened to me?"

I took a step toward my car. He'd already guessed my assumption: a brawl, turf wars, brass knuckles and half-inch steel chain, doing whatever tough guys do in his neighborhood.

"You really want to know?" he said. "I was crossing Thomas Road. Someone hit me. Didn't even slow down. That's what some people do."

He stared at me accusingly. His right eye looked like a piece of raw meat, but his other eye bore into me. He was indicting me. I was the guy in the car who'd run him down. I'd written the laws to get rid of him and his mother, stormed the stinking tenements with pistols drawn and slapped around his countrymen; I'd built the wall brick by brick to keep them out. What did he want from me? Some kind of reparation? An apology? Still, looking down at him, I couldn't quash a knavish guilt I'd been trying to tuck away in some nether region of my mind for the last few weeks.

"I never wanted this to happen," I said. "I hope you understand that. They put me in a bad position. They wanted to shut me down. They wanted to make an example of you. It wasn't personal. You understand? People could have lost their jobs. I have a family." Hector stared up at me. I wanted to ask about Yolanda, find out what had become of her. I wanted to hear she was fine. But I didn't ask. Hector licked his parched lips and looked up at the building. A sharp sliver of moon floated in the eastern sky.

"I'll take you to the hospital," I said.

"And who would pay for it?" He stood and then started limping toward Camelback. "How would I answer their questions?"

My mind was grasping for something. I wanted to help, extend the olive branch.

"Where you going? I can drive you."

He turned to me. His shadow bled across the parking lot and stopped at my feet. He laughed.

"People like you don't go where I go."

Joey was born the next night. No complications. A cramp in the lower back, the drive to the hospital, the blessed relief of the epidural, and then the pushing that seemed to go on for hours. I fed Kendra ice chips, and like an awkward cheerleader intoned encouraging words I felt silly saying: *breathe, push, you're doing fine.* More pushing, and then I saw him, my son, first nothing more than a few slick brown curls on the top of his head, and then a face that looked so serene, a blank slate. I cried. Kendra cried. And later, while she slept, I sat by her bed and drowsily watched the nurse wheel Joey to the nursery. I was exhausted, too, floating between consciousness and sleep, happy and content. I closed my eyes and smiled. I had this pleasant image of my son's life spreading outward from this room, filling our house, a classroom, a college dormitory, filling the whole world. And then

I felt a sudden stupor, a shadow spilling over my thoughts. What came up out of that darkness was an image of Hector, crossing Camelback in a slow, stiff shuffle. My body jolted, my eyes snapped open. Somewhere down the hall I heard a vacuum cleaner. Someone said something in Spanish. Where was Hector going? He'd never answered. Where? I couldn't even imagine.

Friend or Foe

Beyond the Lights

This was when Burger and I were seventeen, before the Supermall and the Muckleshoot Indian Casino turned Auburn into a suburban dump. Back then everyone listened to Nirvana, and everyone wanted to be in a band, and everyone could play at least three power chords and the beginning of "Stairway to Heaven." And for a while that year we hung out with Chad Bingham. Bing most people called him—or asshole or douche bag when he wasn't around.

He was shorter than us, bigger around the chest and belly, with these ferocious blue eyes like propane set alight. A pistol ready to fire or a man standing over a pile of stacked boards with his arm poised above his head—that's the impression Bing gave us. He took karate at the Goju Center in Kent and had even won a few tournaments in Seattle. The trophies in his room proved it. Burger and I would stare at them with reverent wonder. Our parents, always worried about broken bones and concussions, had pushed us into noncontact sports. Tennis. Swimming. Track. We'd look at those trophies, at the faceless plastic men, gold and shiny, caught in the middle of a fierce flying kick or an upward jab, and think, "It's not too late for us. We still have time."

Bing moved from Bellevue at the beginning of our junior year, and his parents bought the biggest house in Highland Meadows, a palace with a racquetball court and an indoor swimming pool. From its glass sunroom that looked over the Green Valley I could see my house through a stand of tall cedars, the mossy roof and faded paint, no bigger than a dollhouse from that distance.

Before Bellevue, Bing had lived in Hong Kong. And before that in Abu Dhabi. He'd been other places, too. Rome, Beijing, Rio de Janeiro.

He'd once seen a man stabbed in a Cairo market. There'd been the metallic flash of the knife right before it sank into the chest, and the fleshy sound of it, something like slicing through a cantaloupe, and then the wild spread of blood. We were eating when he told us this. Maybe at Taco Bell or Herfy's. I don't remember. What I do remember is the quick jolt I felt in my stomach and how Burger turned green.

It was our senior year, our last year before adulthood and that unfamiliar world we'd apprenticed for all our lives. We felt most alive when we were out with Bing or sitting with him in the halogen glare of Trojan Field on a Saturday night as the Auburn High School football team mercilessly charged down the turf and the cheerleaders kicked their tan legs high in the air, shook their gold pom-poms, and shouted things like "Go, Donny, go!" Brooke Barbasolo, Kendra Sweeney, Shannon Palfrey, Cindy Conn, Heidi Sandberg, Hailey McGinnis. Kendra was my and Burger's favorite, and often we discussed what it would be like to kiss her. Burger and I spoke in the hypothetical. We'd never kissed a girl.

Bing was more experienced in these matters. He and Brooke, or so he told us, had been hooking up every couple of weeks at Game Farm Park to make out in a dark corner of the parking lot. But the whole thing was secret because she was dating Brian Schwartz, our second-string quarterback, and if Brian found out there'd be trouble. Of course, Bing assured us he'd take care of Brian if that happened.

He also assured us that Brooke planned to break things off with Brian when the football season ended.

Down on the field, Donny Goodin would smash through the line and run the ball into the end zone, the band would strike up something timeless and inspiring like "Iron Man" or "Smoke on the Water," Kendra would kick her left leg above her head, and I might see a flash of green panties beneath her pleated white skirt. We'd be on our feet, pumping our fists in the air. We'd look over at Bing, his arms crossed, coolly checking out Brooke, his mouth slightly open, and then we'd look at Brooke, ponytail bouncing, teeth radiant, and we believed she was staring at Bing. We'd clap and make strange hooting noises because Bing was making out with Brooke and because we were in love with Kendra and because we were on our way to an undefeated season.

Bing's parents were up in the stands. They told us to call them Larry and Barbara. Together they seemed to orbit a space closer to the gods. Then we saw our parents up there and got depressed. They were forty-something going on fifty-five, bland and pale, our mothers with their bobbed hair and stonewashed jeans and that roll of belly fat and our fathers, with fleshy jowls and billowing sweatpants hiked up practically to their nipples. They chased numbers around spreadsheets all day at Boeing and always feared losing their jobs.

Larry, though, was a partner in a Seattle law firm. He smelled like the ocean and had a sailboat and a speedboat and a cabin on San Juan Island that he promised to take us to. And Barbara, tall and blonde, a former actress who'd once, or so Bing said, been offered the lead role in *The Graduate* but lost it when she wouldn't sleep with the producer. And Barbara's friend was always there. Lydia. She'd been a model at one time, but now she and Barbara owned a clothing boutique in Bellevue. She was tall and blonde and beautiful. When she stood with the crowd and tipped her head back and gave it a little shake that whipped her hair around, I'd elbow Burger, and we'd see all the fathers staring at her. This troubled us: all those married men lusting after this woman!

But then Donny Goodin would score again or Greg Debolt would kick a forty-yard field goal, and we'd be on our feet shouting, and the band would strike up one of those timeless songs. Burger and I felt on those nights that the whole world had condensed into this one moment—the lights and the cheering and the madness, and we knew in a year we'd be out there beyond the lights, in a world we couldn't quite imagine, wearing the white shirts and dark suits we'd been raised to wear. Elder Anderson and Elder Burger. Mormon missionaries. We wanted adventure. "Dear God," we prayed, "send us to Ghana. Send us to Manila. Not Boise. Not Indianapolis."

After the mission there'd be school and marriage and children and the eternities. But we wouldn't do it like our parents. Burger and I vowed that. We wouldn't shrivel up into the tired, upright shells of ourselves and hope for the world beyond. We'd do it like Bing's parents. We promised to never get old and square.

So after the game we'd cruise Auburn and throw things at people or drench them with the fire extinguisher Bing stole from the school gym, a chrome cylinder we pressurized with an air hose at the BP station. And it was all right because everyone was in on the fun.

That's how it was on those nights after the games, the scream of victory still ringing our ears, Burger driving his dad's Ford Taurus station wagon, Bing in the backseat laughing hysterically, and me hanging out the passenger window, the engine roaring and the warm air in my face.

We were searching for a whiff of something profound and timeless in that subterranean night, or at least something puerile and memorable. We'd fly down Lake Holm Road at eighty miles an hour to feel the car lift off the ground when we topped a rise. We'd stare at each other, grinning stupidly, and know we were toeing a thin edge we wanted to see up close without toppling over. The windows were down, and we'd scream into the darkness, flip the car around and do it again. Later we'd settle into a corner booth at Denny's to eat onion rings and drink Dr Pepper. Bing talked. Burger and I listened.

"I'm already a millionaire," Bing told us one night at Denny's. "Or maybe a billionaire." He drank coffee and stared at a spot just above us where the ceiling met the wall. He had a wild look and spoke in a voice so low Burger and I had to lean in to hear. "Maybe I shouldn't even tell you this," he said. "You promise not to tell anyone?" Of course we promised. We licked our lips and felt our eyeballs go dry.

He told us how back in the seventies his dad had saved the ancestral land of this Peruvian Indian tribe from some greedy American oil company, and to show their gratitude this tribe gave him a cave full of gold. His dad had seen the cave with his own eyes, walls of pure gold from the floor to ceiling, and all he had to do was toss a rock against the wall and enough gold would flake off to buy a Mercedes. Then these Indians told his dad that they'd guard the cave until he could come back for it someday.

We had forgotten the onion rings in front of us. Burger was in a trance. "And why"—his voice cracked, he panted—"and why didn't they want the gold?"

Bing was patient. He spoke slowly. He knew we didn't understand much of the world outside Auburn. "These people live in dirt," he said. "They eat worms and think a bracelet made from crocodile teeth is high fashion. What would they do with gold?"

Then Bing told us how his dad said he could have every ounce of that gold. There was a map in a locked metal box under Bing's bed. His dad gave it to him years ago.

Bing looked at me and then at Burger. "It'll be back-breaking work," he said. "We'll have to buy donkeys and shovels, and we can't tell anyone. They'd slit your throats." Bing, of course, wasn't worried about himself. He knew karate. He was worried about us, and that was touching. He'd pay us a million apiece to help him. Maybe more. He wanted to know if we were in, if we could endure the jungle heat and eating bugs and fighting off anyone who wanted the gold. Of course we could. So it was decided: Burger and I would save our money and leave the week after graduation, stay a year, and then return for our missions.

I started running the track after school and doing fifty push-ups every night before bed. I bought a set of dumbbells and did curls until my arms burned. Burger loaded a backpack with river rock and hiked the narrow trails around Flaming Geyser Park, and then did wind sprints on the lawn until he puked. We rented Bruce Lee movies and practiced kicks and commando rolls on my front lawn. We punched and kicked couch cushions in my backyard until my mom yelled from the window that we'd ruin the leather. We poured over a Spanish phrase book I found at Goodwill. *Mucho gusto. Dónde está el baño? Necesito un medico*!

Two weeks into our training, Burger called. He'd just finished thirty minutes of wind sprints at Flaming Geyser. "Do you think

Bing's dad is telling the truth?" he asked. There was a thickness in his voice. He gulped for air. "I mean, do you think there's really gold down there?"

"There's a map," I said. "Bing told us. We just follow the map."

One Saturday night in early November we were out in the Taurus station wagon. We had the fire extinguisher, two Super Soakers, and a five-gallon bucket of water balloons. We were ready to drench anyone or anything we happened upon: man, woman, child, dog. My fingers were sticky. I'd just eaten three Hostess fruit pies and felt a dizzying clarity from all the sugar. Burger drove, seat reclined, hand looped over the steering wheel. Bing sat up front with the extinguisher. I was in the back.

We were at the stoplight on 2nd and Auburn Way, and right there in front of the Korean dry cleaner we saw this woman talking to a guy in a blue Ford F-150. This would be hilarious. We knew it. All we had to do was call her over. Then we'd drench her.

So Burger pulled up across the street, and then Bing was half out the window, rapping his knuckles against the car roof and whistling. This pissed off the guy in the Ford. I could see his face, freckled with a thin blond mustache. He told the woman to get in the truck, but she was looking our way, and then the guy glared at us, spit out the window, and sped away. And it was just the woman there.

Bing told us to watch. He told us this would be hilarious.

The woman slowly walked over, stumbling across the street as if it weren't asphalt at all but thick mud she was navigating through. She wasn't a little thing, not at all, but kind of full-figured, Botticelli's Venus emerging from the sea, round cheeks and a pile of red curly hair falling into her face. She wore bleached jeans and a thick maroon sweater and had no shoes on. When she passed in front of the car she stopped and squinted into the bright lights before walking around to the passenger side.

By this time Bing was back in his seat, passing the extinguisher's nozzle from one hand to the other, as if doing some kind of exercise.

The woman leaned over and looked at us for about thirty seconds before saying anything. There was a tattoo on her left hand, just above the thumb, no bigger than a dime, a red heart with the letters PF written underneath. "You won't hurt me?" she asked. The words dragged out of her mouth, almost incomprehensible, each syllable a trembling thing.

Bing said we wouldn't hurt her, and then he looked at us and told the woman that Burger and I were Mormon, which was as good as being a pacifist, and that we had never hurt anyone in our lives and were actually quite accustomed to being persecuted. In fact, he said we welcomed persecution. The woman leaned in a little closer, squinted some more, and told us that if we were Mormon then we'd better give her a ride to Tacoma because that would be the Christian thing to do. Her upper lip caught on a crooked tooth, and a burst of wind blew wisps of that thick red hair in her face. She brushed the hair behind her ears and went on about some guy she met at a bar on Main Street and how he'd stolen her shoes and purse and left her in the gravel parking lot of a junk yard on C Street and how now she needed a ride to Tacoma and how she didn't have any money but she was sure some kind of arrangement could be made. And as she went on, Bing kept turning to Burger and me, kept smiling and winking and nodding his head and mouthing words I couldn't make out. But I understood that this was hilarious, the funniest thing in the world, and how later we'd laugh about this at Denny's, pound the table with our fists and recount our various perspectives on what had happened. I could see Bing gripping the silver nozzle, his knuckles white.

Bing cut the woman off. "We're not going to Tacoma," he said, "but I'll give you ten bucks if you take off your shirt." He took the money from his wallet and waved it in the woman's face. She swallowed, bit her lower lip.

And then so quickly, like a jerky splice in a film, she was topless. Breasts, nipples, pale white skin. I knew I should be feeling this glimpse of the exposed female form in the deepest parts of my reproductive tract—but I felt only a dull ache in my stomach. Stretch marks, like the tiny cracks in porcelain, spread across her stomach, and looking at them, I couldn't help think of my mother, how so many years ago we took baths together and how she washed my small toes and fingers and sang silly songs, and I remembered staring at her body, at the curve of her stomach and breasts, and the pale lines there. As a child, I assumed they were from some kind of injury.

Bing, throwing out a booming cackle that filled the car, doubled over with laughter, and the woman just stood there, eyeballs rolling back in her head. Then Bing reached for the maroon sweater in the woman's hands and yanked at it. The woman, suddenly lucid, pulled back. Bing raised the nozzle and sprayed her in the face, and as if by magic two black streams ran from her eyes, down her cheeks, and between her breasts. She screamed and stumbled backward, dropping the sweater. Bing shouted at Burger to go. The car jumped forward, the tires screamed, and there was a momentary sensation of moving sideways. Then I turned and saw the woman collapsed on the curb, knees to her chest, her body red in the glow of the tail lights. Bing didn't look back.

We moved quickly up D Street, and Bing was still laughing, still holding the nozzle. He aimed it at two figures who materialized in the headlights, two men, heads shaved to the skull, thick black boots and jeans rolled up to their boot tops. They didn't turn until the first stream of water lashed their backs, and when they did turn, Bing hit them in the face with another volley. There was cursing and the beat of those heavy black boots, and we were off again into the night.

We ended up at Les Gove Park.

The parking lot was empty. Not a soul for miles, it seemed. It was late, past eleven, and I was done for the night. Burger was done, too. He slouched in the driver's seat, resting his head against the steering wheel, and for a moment I thought he was praying.

I couldn't stop thinking about this woman, so tired and wasted, those eyes, that hair, the paleness of her skin—and no shoes. I thought if someone gave her a bed she might sleep for days, maybe weeks, and when she woke up, I wondered who she'd be.

"Who do you think she was?" I asked. Bing, still in the front seat, his face in shadows, said, "Who knows?" Then he added quickly, "Who cares?"

A song played on the radio, something deliciously catchy that we'd never hear again without thinking of that night. Bing laughed as he replayed the scene with the woman, giving particular attention to her ringing falsetto as he yanked at the sweater and then the cold shock of the water as it caught her in the eyes. The windows were down and a sharp breeze pulled at the leafless alders overhanging the parking lot. I smelled something in the air, something wet and earthy that made me shiver.

I heard the quick scrape of thick rubber soles on asphalt and then saw a shadow move across the car. I looked up. They were there, the two characters Bing had hosed, their T-shirts and jeans still wet from the assault. In the weak light I saw the swell of pectorals pushing at the thin cotton fabric and the hard veins running up their arms. They were breathing heavily, just staring down at us. One said, "These the dicks, Mickey?"

There was no response, only the blur of hands through the open windows, grabbing for us. Burger reached for the keys still in the ignition, a futile effort. One bad character had him by the hair, slamming his face into the steering wheel. I had my own problems in the backseat, fending off a pair of thick hands. I lay on my back and kicked fiercely, but then I felt those hands cinch around my ankles and pull.

I was going through the window, my shirt piling up around my nipples, the small knob that locks the door gouging my right kidney and then the tender spaces between each rib. I was on the ground, knees curled to my chest, hands covering my head, looking under the car at the shocks, at the muffler, at all the grime impacted there. There was no pleading, no quick apology or cry for mercy. The fall had knocked the air out of my lungs. I could barely breathe. But then I had the feeling that these were men of action, wronged, and there to teach a lesson. They spat out a string of repeated profanities as they wailed on us. It sounded like a chant, like a war cry.

Steel-toed kicks to the ribs, fists hard as stones pounding my back. Then the passenger door swung open and I saw Bing's Adidas planted there on the asphalt. I felt relief was only moments away. I waited for something spectacular, for Bing to vault the hood and lay out the bad characters with a fierce roundhouse. Instead, those black Adidas beat a quick retreat into the darkness.

The thrashing went on a minute more, but we were already numb to it. My nose dripped blood. I could taste it thick and coppery in my mouth. I thought one of my teeth might be chipped. Burger's nose dripped blood, too. There was a gash across his forehead, and the bridge of his nose looked swollen. I felt such pity for him in that moment, such brotherly love as we both lay there panting. The bad characters stood over us, panting, too, blood on their knuckles and pant legs. Then they turned to the car.

Not wanting to attract attention, I barely looked, but I heard it, the dull thump of boots on the car's metal body, the sharp snap of the windshield wipers. One guy bounced on the car roof as if it were a trampoline, and the other heaved a metal garbage can against the rear window. They grinned wildly, howling and cheering as the car shed glass. And then they were gone.

We stood on shaky limbs, wiped our bloody noses and mouths, and surveyed the afflicted car. The mirror on the driver's side dangled by two thin yellow wires. Bits of safety glass twinkled against the deep black of the parking lot. Burger, his eyes large dark pools, had his hand clamped over his mouth. A muffled profanity squeezed through. We circled the car, touched the cratered body, and said nothing. The shock of having to tell Burger's parents, the lie we'd have to invent, had distracted us from our bruised ribs and aching heads.

We opened the doors, brushed the glass from the seats and eased in, feeling the scream and complaint of every muscle and bone. Burger started the car and put it in reverse, whimpering as he turned to look out the rear window, half of which was scattered over the backseat. It was in that moment that Bing emerged from the darkness. We'd almost forgotten him. His sudden return had a visceral effect on me. My teeth ground together, my right eyelid trembled.

Bing ducked into the backseat with a sheepish grin on his face. "I was gonna jump in," he said. "I was waiting for the right moment." He stammered, gaped at the blood on our faces. "It happened so fast."

We said nothing.

"I was looking for a phone"—Bing's head swiveled between us, his hands beat the air—"to call the police." He made a fist and ground it into his palm. "My dad knows some people in the police department. They'll find these assholes and put them in jail. And the car. You'll have enough money in a year to buy three new Cadillacs."

Burger laughed, a new kind of laughter, deep and bitter and savage. "You're full of shit," he said, wiping his eyes and fighting for composure. "And your dad is too."

Bing's lips moved spasmodically, but with no sound. Then Burger turned to Bing. He wasn't laughing anymore. His cheeks and eyes were dark with shadows, and when he spoke, I didn't recognize his voice. "Your dad's a cheat and a liar. I saw him and Lydia at Flaming Geyser Park. They were in his car. She was touching his face. They were kissing."

Burger smiled, just sat there and smiled at Bing. I could see it in Burger's face, the pure thrill of those words as they hit their mark, more destructive and painful than a fist to the jaw. I felt the thrill, too. I wanted those words to be true. I wanted to hurt Bing, and that, even now, is what shocks me most, not the insincerity and paradox of Larry's infidelity, but the pain I wanted to inflict on Bing.

Bing made a puffing noise. Something caught in his throat, and then he was crying, his cheeks wet and shining. "It's not true," he said. He repeated the phrase over and over, eyes sloppy and pleading and fixed on Burger as if all Burger had to do was take it back and everything would be fine.

We drove to the high school, Bing whimpering all the way and wiping his nose. When we pulled up to Bing's car, Burger idled there listening to the hum of the engine. Bing's eyes bounced between us as if he wanted us to say something, but we didn't, not until Burger told him to get the hell out of the car.

Bing stood there in the road as we drove away. We watched him recede, red in the glow of the taillights, and marveled at his transformation, at the doughy belly overhanging his belt and the flab under his chin. We marveled that we'd ever believed anything he said.

This was back when Auburn had one high school and two junior highs, the year before Walmart and Lowe's erected their fortresses off the 167, before Main Street deteriorated into a row of empty store fronts with dark, dusty windows. Back then you could ditch your bike anywhere along Lake Holm Road and hike through the woods without a stray golf ball knocking you in the skull. The football team was undefeated that year and so was the basketball team. And all of us laughed when that lunatic from Enumclaw dive-bombed our graduation ceremony in a Cessna, and we couldn't understand then why our parents were so uptight about it or why the police arrested him.

Maybe we were too hard on Bing. This was before Burger and I were missionaries, before we were young husbands and young fathers, employees and breadwinners, before we understood that most of our lives would be spent in the dim glow of some distant victory, pretending we were something we weren't and knowing that out there beyond the glow of the stadium lights there was, and always would be, a shadow hunting us down.

The Righteous Road

My mom held her hand over the phone. "It's Reed," she whispered.

I took the phone and leaned against the countertop. "Hello," I said. "Hello."

"What, Derrick? No call?" Reed asked.

"I didn't know you were home." I lied.

In November Reed sent a practically illegible postcard. He was always sending postcards, from Istanbul, Mumbai, Munich, Hong Kong, all written in a sharp, hurried scrawl. *Let's get together over Christmas. It'll be like old times.* I'd studied the postcard: a squalid open market in Jerusalem, bins of dried fruit and lentils, skinless goat and sheep carcasses suspended from steel hooks.

Then there were his letters, as long as novellas, self-aggrandizing rants stuffed in manila envelopes he'd decorated with intricate and baffling designs. His message was always the same: the minute details of his service among the impoverished and downtrodden masses, and his grandiose plans for a future that had us saving the world from tyranny and environmental annihilation. I couldn't finish the letters, nor could I respond with equal enthusiasm. The letters were too didactic, trying to persuade me to recapture some embellished memories from years past. Unlike Reed, I'd grown up, moved on, gone to college. I was in my last year of law school at Brigham Young University. I was engaged.

"I knew you wouldn't get the postcard," Reed said. "They were going through my mail. Israeli secret service. The *Mossad*. Sometimes they'd follow me. But that's life." He said this as if the inconvenience of wiretaps and surveillance were a fact of his workaday world. "What's important is that you're here," Reed said. "There's someone who needs our help. Eight at my house. You in?"

I could only guess who this somebody might be: the Palestinians, Mexican border crossers, old-growth Douglas firs, the spotted owl, humpback whales? I imagined having to endure one of Reed's windy, vainglorious speeches, a call to action to save the oppressed or right some ecological wrong, and me sitting there nodding ecstatically as if I still devoutly believed in the cause. I was ready to tell Reed I had to catch a plane in the morning, which was true. I was flying to Aspen to spend the weekend with my fiancée, Cassie, and her family. But the thought of another night playing Scrabble with my parents while my dad grumbled about his irritable bowels and diminishing retirement seemed unbearable. Worse, I imagined Reed showing up on our doorstep.

"I'll be there," I said.

My mom was on me the second I hung up. Behind her, the Christmas tree winked on and off in a way that hurt my eyes.

"I never liked Reed," she said, "even when you were little boys. Always a bad influence. And all that mischief in high school. I never believed you thought it up yourself. His parents had a handful. Edna Swenson still calls me. She cries about him. Did you know that? She wonders where she and Bob went wrong. She blames herself."

"Boys will be boys." I said this to get a rise from her, not because I believed it. I was of the opinion, and had been for years, that Reed needed to move beyond the perpetual adolescence he lived in.

"But when do boys grow up?" my mom said. She began rearranging the nativity on the coffee table. "You grew up. Maybe you can talk some sense into him." She pointed a shepherd at me. "Tell him to go to college and stop giving his parents grief. Tell him to go back to church. He's still young enough to serve a mission. It's Edna's dream."

"I'm not going to talk some sense into him," I said. I didn't want the responsibility of steering Reed back into the fold. Besides, Reed worshipped Mother Earth. His congregation convened in the tops of trees while angry loggers cursed from below, or outside third world sweat shops where the oppressed toiled for a nickel an hour. His sacrament was a thick joint and cheap wine.

"You just be careful over there," my mom said. "I can't imagine he's changed much. Still the same old Reed."

Her concern annoyed me. As if Reed had any influence on me. He was a vestige from another life, an adolescent, idealistic incarnation of myself I would never relive.

We grew up in the same wooded subdivision outside Auburn, Washington, had the same teachers at Lake View Elementary, attended the same ward. The sand box, Sunday school, Cub Scouts, tee-ball. When didn't I know Reed?

He always had this deeper ecological and humanitarian consciousness. Our Sunday school teachers, sweet old ladies who brought us oatmeal cookies, stared incredulously as Reed decried the cruelty of Mosaic animal sacrifice or questioned the goodness of a God who required the massacre of every Canaanite living in the Promised Land. At twelve, Reed's first youth talk in sacrament meeting was a five-minute criticism of God's command to Adam and Eve to subdue the earth and have dominion over it. "Why can't all His creations just have an equal relationship?" Reed asked from the pulpit, his voice quivering with emotion. "Why can't everything just be free and happy without people messing up the forests and the air?"

When we were fifteen, Reed's ecological sense found a focus. It was one of those boring summer nights, nothing to do but sit in Reed's living room and flip through channels until we were catatonic. The only thing on was a Greenpeace paid advertisement asking for donations to protest the Icelandic seal hunts. I watched in horror as a man in a blue fur-lined parka clubbed a pod of yelping harp seals to death. The saliva drained from my mouth and a nauseating weight bloomed in my guts. I wanted to turn the channel and forget this injustice, find a brainless comedy to purge the disquieting image of the doomed seals. Reed made a choking sound. His lower lip quivered, and glistening lines of snot oozed from both nostrils. Tears streamed down his cheeks. I pretended not to notice.

Then in the middle of all that slaughter, the deathblows and the freshly skinned pelts, the camera shifted to four men dragging an activist across the blood-spattered ice. Tall, with a blond beard and fierce blue eyes, the activist chanted something about stopping the slaughter. Lars Norgard, we later learned, Greenpeace activist and captain of the *Sea Shepherd*, a man of mythical proportions who'd made a name for himself ramming a dozen whaling ships.

Wiping the snot from his nose, Reed said, as if in a trance, "That's what I want to be."

Reed called a toll-free number that flashed on the TV screen, and in a couple of weeks some brochures came in the mail. We poured over each color photograph: the *Sea Shepherd* slicing through the glacial, turbulent North Atlantic; hippie kids chaining themselves to the bows of fishing boats; and Lars Norgard, with his thick blond beard, standing on the *Sea Shepherd's* bridge, barking commands into a CB radio as he stared down a menacing Russian whaling ship. What more could two fifteen-year-old boys want? Adventure, danger, heroes and villains, the open seas. We wrote Lars and volunteered our services. We'd do anything: scrub toilets, cook food, wash laundry, whatever he needed.

Lars actually wrote back. We sniffed the envelope and thought we could smell the briny sea. While applauding our ecological maturity and commitment to such a noble cause, Lars said that by law we'd have to wait until we were eighteen. Until then, if we really wanted to stop the bastards, we should send money for fuel. "Keep believing and continue the fight," he wrote. "Patience. When the time comes, I'll have two spots on the *Sea Shepherd* for my eco-warriors." The words thrilled us.

We must have gotten on a mailing list. The pamphlets and newsletters filled Reed's mailbox: Animal Liberation Front, Amnesty International, PETA, Doctors without Borders, the Sierra Club. Shocked and sickened, we stared at the sharp color images of clear-cut wastelands and veal calves wallowing in their own feces and skeletal Somalis with distended bellies. Before, such abject suffering and unchecked destruction had existed only in the abstract, a brief image on the evening news. My parents had shielded me, I knew, and now I wanted to do something about all this misery and devastation, something more than praying for the sick and afflicted or cleaning out flower vases at Mountain View Cemetery for church service projects. All that seemed ridiculously inconsequential when I considered the dying whales and the vanquished ancient forests and the starving Somalis.

When we could finally drive, we skipped school one Friday to check out an animal experimentation protest Reed saw advertised in the *Seattle Weekly*. There were about a hundred people there, chanting, waving signs, and marching in front of a towering glass and steel skyscraper in downtown Bellevue. Someone dressed in a fluffy rabbit suit splashed with red paint was writhing on the sidewalk. One man wore a dog costume and had Vaseline smeared over his eyes. He howled mournfully as a woman led him around by the paw. Truthfully, Reed and I thought it was a bit much, until we looked at the literature a protester handed us and saw the lab photos of terrified beagles hanging from their paws, kittens with electrodes protruding from their skulls, and a chimpanzee in an oxygen mask running on a caged treadmill. All that suffering so Meyer Chemical could sell us lip balm and antifungal cream. The protesters' outrage was contagious. Reed and I walked up to a middle-aged man in dreadlocks who seemed in charge and asked if we could help. Smiling and then giving us both a bro hug, he handed us signs. For the rest of the afternoon we marched, blocked sidewalk traffic, and loudly upbraided anyone who dared enter the building.

After that, we were sneaking up to Seattle a couple of times a month to march and pass out literature at anti-fur rallies or to knock doors for Amnesty International. At night we'd go out with other activists to spray-paint butcher shops and furriers with pithy slogans like *Feed it, don't eat it* or *Are clothes to kill for?* After, we'd hang out in some grimy apartment in the University District or near Capitol Hill and listen to stories of rousing environmental and humanitarian escapades while Phish played in the background and a thick joint and a jug of wine made the rounds. We partook because these were the fruits of the earth, or so they told us, a shared sacrament for nature's children meant to enlighten the mind and strengthen the body. If I experienced any guilt after that first toke, these assurances certainly mitigated it, as did my budding awareness that as an only child I felt controlled and smothered. I wanted an identity apart from Mormonism and my parents' conservative politics. My parents bored me. No hobbies, no friends they went out with, no interest in music and art. If that was righteousness, I didn't want it.

Soon, Reed and I stopped eating meat and dairy. We refused to wear our black leather church shoes, refused to wear any brand that exploited its workers in third world sweatshops.

At home, my parents said little about my new-found activism, probably believing it would pass. Reed, however, felt morally compelled to win his sister and parents over to his way of thinking. He saw their ecological and humanitarian apathy as rooted in what he called the naïve and narrow-minded strictures of Mormonism. Suddenly, Reed's rhetoric burned with anti-religious sentiments: religion as a social construct, as a mental illness, as the opium of the masses. He could go on for hours, until even I couldn't take it anymore. His home became a den of acrimony, a constant tension simmering just below the surface, erupting now and then in screaming and vague threats. Reed refused to attend church and early morning seminary. This appealed to me, too, for no other reason than that I longed for more sleep. My parents, probably sensing Reed's influence, offered unrestricted use of my dad's old Plymouth Reliant and a Shell gas card if I didn't miss a day of church or seminary. Even Reed liked the idea. Without a car, he reasoned, how would we get to Seattle?

One Monday in January of our senior year, Reed didn't show up for school. At lunch, I called his house. No one answered. When I got home that afternoon, my parents sat solemnly on the living room couch. My mom dabbed at her red, weepy eyes with a crumpled Kleenex. My dad, who shouldn't have been home for another two hours, stood and pointed to the love seat. "Derrick, we need to talk," he said. My heart pounded.

He said Sister Swenson had called that morning. Reed and two activists had been arrested in Seattle Sunday afternoon for vandalizing an Albertson's meat counter. But there was more. Brother and Sister Swenson, distraught and suspicious after receiving this news, had gone through Reed's drawers and discovered a joint and a bag of dried mushrooms. "You know anything about those?" my dad asked. "Are you and Reed using drugs?"

Staring at our beige carpet, I denied everything, denied vehemently while suddenly realizing my parents knew. I was sure.

Reed was now on a plane to New Mexico, my dad said, where he'd spend the next ten weeks in a wilderness treatment program for drug addiction and behavioral issues. He insisted, at least while Reed was gone, that I take a break from the activism and from our little cadre of hippie friends at school. Now I'd eat lunch with the kids from church. Did I understand?—my dad wanted to know—or did he and my mom need to go upstairs and rummage through my drawers and closet? I stared at his polished Wingtips and nodded quickly.

The next day at school, the church kids—all bores and blind followers of the faith, Reed and I thought—invited me to eat lunch with them, an invitation arranged, I was sure, by my dad and Bishop McKinley. I accepted their invitation, hoping it might allay some of my parents' suspicions. And I'll admit, after two years of fiercely debating the environmental or humanitarian issue *du jour* over lunch with Reed and our friends, I actually enjoyed the cheery, inconsequential conversations about church dances, BYU football, and future mission calls. I sat with them for a month, though I never told Reed.

Reed's first postcard came two weeks after his abrupt departure. "Living off the fat of the land," he wrote. "Stars so pretty. Grateful to the Creator for all good things. Searching for a heart at peace." A week later another postcard: "At harmony with the world. Love and respect for all people." He'd included an enigmatic postscript, a quote from Edward Albee's *The Monkey Wrench Gang*, a book we'd read at least three times. The postscript said: "Because we like the taste of freedom, comrades. Because we like the smell of danger."

It wasn't a surprise, then, at least to me, when Reed escaped.

After a search of the area around the camp yielded no Reed, the Sheriff's department got involved, blazing out into the high desert on motorcycles and ATVs, even in a helicopter flown up from Albuquerque. Search and rescue volunteers came from Santa Fe. With no sign of Reed after three days, his parents flew to New Mexico. The ward fasted and prayed for Reed's safe return. My parents, I'm sure assuming Reed was dead, asked if I'd like to meet with a therapist. Not necessary, I told them, believing Reed was out there living his wilderness dream, holed up in a warm shelter, feasting on pine nuts and cattails as he meditated the hours away. But as the days passed, I considered the possibility that Reed might be gone. At night, worried and unable to sleep, I found myself kneeling at my bedside, something I hadn't done in a long time, praying for my friend's safe return. I somehow knew, with an assurance I couldn't articulate, more a feeling than anything else, that Reed was all right.

And then a week later Reed called his parents from Pueblo, Colorado. Incredibly, he'd endured the freezing, high-desert night and walked fifty miles to the interstate, then hitchhiked the 350 miles to Pueblo. He was staying with some guy who was president of the local clean air conservation group.

Reed's parents drove to Pueblo and pleaded with him to finish the treatment program. He refused. He wanted to go home. His parents wouldn't hear of it. Reed had strained the family to the point of rupture. They quickly reached a compromise with him, one that showed their desperation. Until the end of the school year, they'd rent a studio apartment for Reed near the high school, pay the utilities, and give him a food allowance. He could come home once a week for Sunday dinner. Not a bad arrangement, Reed thought.

Every day after school we smoked weed at his apartment, and Reed would often articulate his vision of our lives after graduation, how we'd travel the world over in search of perilous humanitarian and ecological causes to throw ourselves into. It was talk, or so I thought—the impractical, idealistic machinations of a young man on the cusp of adulthood. Realistically, I saw us at Green River Community College the next year, done with the weed and the booze, hitting the books, and then at nineteen, doing what had been ingrained in us from birth by cheery primary songs and a thousand talks and Sunday school lessons—the mission. I'd meant to bring it up with Reed: the mission as an altruistic adventure, two years serving the indigent gentry of some third world backwater, learning their language, teaching them to love one another. What was wrong with that? I also understood the unspoken stigma we'd bear by not going.

Though I hadn't told Reed, I was tired of the Seattle activists and their scene. Loud, pushy, self-righteous, they disliked almost everything and would go on and on about anarchy and environmental destruction as if they knew nothing else. Ragged clothes and bad teeth, many looked indistinguishable from the homeless and unemployed begging dollars at freeway off-ramps and downtown intersections. I didn't want the ascetic's life, nor did I aspire to excess and luxury. I wanted a few comforts, a life equal to or a little better than my parents'. A decent home for my family. Maybe a nice car. Nothing wrong with that.

But if anything, Reed was becoming more extreme, more dedicated to the cause. He had other plans for us.

It was a Friday at the end of May, two weeks to graduation, when he waved a handwritten letter in my face and said, "You want out of this hole? Here's your ticket." We were at his apartment, smoking a joint. Kurt Cobain screamed from the stereo. I squinted at the letter through a pall of smoke.

"Freedom and adventure. Saving the world," Reed said. "Right? Everything we've talked about for the last three years."

Reed, always audacious, always sniffing out the next adventure, had written Lars Norgard to remind him of his promise, and then, to prove we were ready for a life of activism, he'd detailed our activities of the last three years and explained we were eager to take things to the next level. Lars wrote back. We were in luck. There were two spots on the *Sea Shepherd*, but we'd have to act quickly. He'd be docked at the Tacoma Marina for a couple of hours on Monday, June 13th. He then warned us that this was the most dangerous work in the world, and for that reason he couldn't guarantee our safety. Reed read those words, smiled, and then read them again.

I feigned excitement for the next two weeks as we bought rucksacks from the army surplus store in Seattle and stuffed them with everything Lars said we needed: wool pants and sweaters, rain gear, lug-soled boots, waders, sunscreen. I smiled as we concocted our plan to meet that Monday morning at the bus stop behind JCPenney. I'd leave a note on my bed telling my parents our plan, park the Reliant on Main Street, and then we'd take the bus to Tacoma. I praised the soundness of the plan, all the while knowing I never intended to meet Reed.

That Monday I lay in bed and listened to the phone ring and ring and then go to the answering machine. I was alone, my dad at work, my mom gone to a church quilting project.

"Where are you?" Reed's voice boomed through the answering machine. "Derrick!" He called again and again. I heard him through the pillow I'd put over my head. Finally, I picked up the phone. I owed Reed at least that.

"You sleep in?" he shouted. "Are you sick?"

I cleared my throat. "I'm not sure. . . ." I struggled to finish the sentence. "That life— I'm not sure I want that life." I tried to explain: the transient, hand-to-mouth existence, the pessimism and never-ending activism. "I don't want to give up being Mormon," I told Reed. "I mean, I thought after all this we'd go on missions."

"Missions?" Reed said. He seemed confused. "Why would we go on missions?" And then he drew in a sharp breath. "You believe—" he said slowly, "you believe everything they taught us."

I believed, believed weakly, I knew, perhaps believed through association only, a subconscious absorption of faith as I slept through church and early morning seminary. I believed, maybe, because my parents believed, because despite all their buttoned-up, conservative stuffiness they'd loved me selflessly and unconditionally. I imagined that God, if anything, might be an extension of them. I wondered if the church would let me go on a mission, after all the weed and the alcohol and the vandalism done in the name of saving the planet. I'd have to make amends. Tell my parents everything. Meet weekly with Bishop McKinley.

"I won't even get into how ridiculous it all is," Reed said. I could hear the disgust in his voice. "Angels and gold plates. But that's not even the worse part. It's the culture, Derrick. The Mormon factory. You go on that mission and you walk straight in, and when you come out, you're just like them. You'll dress like them and think like them and talk like them. You'll live in your little bubble. You see that, Derrick? Is that what you want?"

"But what if we do it differently?" I said. The idea suddenly came to me. I held the portable phone tightly to my ear and paced the living room. "Not like our parents. What if we did it our way and still believed?"

"Do it differently?" Reed said. "It's not in the program, Derrick. They don't want that."

I heard the hiss of air breaks, and then a monotone voice crackle over a speaker.

"Derrick," Reed said. His voice trembled. "Come on. There's still time. You don't think we can do some good? There's other ways to do good."

I felt a rawness in the back of my throat. "I'm sorry," I said.

That night I called Reed's dad. There was no anger or accusations. Brother Swenson thanked me, and that was it. Reed was eighteen. What could Brother Swenson do? I knew the truth. He was glad Reed was gone.

I spent the year at Green River Community College, attended the stake singles' ward, made restitution and repented for everything I'd done. I received a mission call to serve in Rio de Janeiro. After, I enrolled at BYU and earned a degree in political science. And then law school. I hadn't seen Reed in seven years, but in that time, a month had never passed without a letter or postcard from him.

At eight o'clock, I told my parent's that I'd be home in an hour. Reed's postcard sat on the kitchen countertop, a burst of color against a grid of small beige tiles. I took it, tossing it in the outside trash bin as I walked to the car.

Within minutes I stood on Reed's doorstep. Loud Arabic music rattled the windows, strings and a high androgynous voice locked in a repetitive groove. I knocked hard and waited.

The music stopped, and then a moment later Reed stood in the doorway, smiling. He wore a Greenpeace T-shirt, faded jeans, and a white knitted beanie. "Seven years," he said, taking my arm and pulling me into the house. "Seven years and rarely a letter. And look at you now: the lawyer in embryo. You gonna stick it to those fat cats in their corporate towers?"

"Sure," I said. I could only imagine the selfless narrative Reed had conjured up for me, the rabid environmental lawyer saving the world from greedy land developers and wicked industrialists intent on melting the ice caps and decimating every forest. Actually, I was leaning toward corporate law. My dad agreed. The hours were long, but the money was good. The previous two summers I'd clerked in Latham and Watkins' Los Angeles office, and I was optimistic they'd offer me a job after law school. I wanted stability. I wanted to provide a comfortable life for my family. I wanted to be a partner. But I knew these achievements meant nothing to Reed. He'd think there was no adventure in it, nothing of the bravado and altruism we'd dreamed about and discussed years ago while smoking a joint in his apartment. Worse, he'd think I had become one of them, sold out for the all-powerful dollar.

"And you, the world traveler," I said, because I knew that's what Reed wanted, a little opening to gush about his adventures, to sing his environmental consciousness and deep empathy for others.

"I've been a few places," he said, ushering me toward the couch. "But it's good to be home, right? The old stomping ground. You want something to eat or drink?" he asked. "Some juice or cookies?"

"No, I've eaten. I just came to say hello."

He insisted. "Come on. What can I get you?"

"Really, I'm fine," I said.

"You have to try this tamarind nectar I brought back from Gaza," Reed said.

He was halfway to the kitchen before I could protest.

"How are your parents?" I asked, hoping they'd materialize from somewhere. I was uncomfortable around Reed. After so many years, he felt like a stranger.

"Still believing their conservative conspiracy theories," Reed shouted from the kitchen. "Still praying Reagan will rise from the grave. God help us all. Actually, they took my sister and her husband to Crystal Mountain for the night. They're sick of me already."

Reed returned with a plate of baklava and two glasses brimming with an opaque liquid. He handed me a glass and then set the plate on the coffee table. He took a long drink, smacking his lips and looking at me expectantly. The liquid had the sheen of motor oil and smelled slightly fermented. I took a sip and cringed as the sweetness hit my fillings.

"Delicious," Reed said, before emptying his glass.

"It's different," I said, taking another small drink. I looked around the living room, at the beige carpet and the black leather Lazyboy. Nothing had changed in ten years. In fact, I was sitting on the same brown microfiber sectional where we'd first seen Lars Norgard protesting the seal hunts. "How's Lars Norgard?" I asked. "What's he like?"

"A phony," Reed said quickly and unequivocally. He picked at something under his thumbnail. "'Fuel to help us get the bastards,' my ass. The man's a gambling addict. And"—Reed knocked his knuckles together—"he's a carnivore. An environmental phony. I was done with him a long time ago."

"Well, it's good to see you," I said. "Really good." I tried to think of more to say, to dredge up some nugget from years ago to carry the conversation, some innocuous memory we could bat around for a minute. I asked about Israel.

"Palestine," Reed said. "The Zionist propaganda wants to erase history, like no one lived there before 1948. Gaza and the West Bank are concentration camps. Genocide. People dying every day and no one hears about it. I wanted to change that."

I was confused, but not surprised. "I thought you were studying Arabic. Didn't you mention that in a letter?"

"Just a cover," Reed said. He put his hand over his mouth and laughed. "My ticket into the country. A lowly student at Birzeit University. My mom was thrilled. I didn't tell her that I was a human shield with this group called *Adalah*. And then the Zionist pricks caught wind of what I was doing. Israeli Secret Service. They think I'm an insurgent. Can you believe that?"

"You were a human shield?" I said. I thought of long-haired, wild-eyed hippies throwing themselves in front of bulldozers. "Don't people die doing that?" I could only imagine the swollen image Reed had of himself: the solitary, undeterred student halting that massive tank in Tiananmen Square, the revolutionary, a savior to the oppressed.

"It happens," Reed said stoically. "It's war and war has its martyrs. Put your bodies upon the gears and upon the wheels, upon the levers, upon all the apparatus." Reed shoved a piece of baklava in his mouth. "At Ramallah and Nablus we stopped the Israelis. We built roadblocks. But that's not all. Remember how I always said I wanted to fight in a revolution?"

Reed was on a roll now, warming to the subject. When he reached for another chunk of baklava, I glanced at my watch. I thought of letting him go on for another fifteen minutes before I made my exit.

"None of that passive-aggressive shit," Reed said. "I wanted the real thing. Tear gas and Molotov cocktails. I knew these guys in *Hamas* and sometimes I'd go out with them at night. Patrol, they called it. What a rush. I even got something to show for it." He inched up his sleeve to reveal a gauze bandage wrapped tightly around his bicep, and then he unwound it with a practiced dalliance. As the gauze fell away, I saw a crusted red gash no longer than an inch. "The kid standing next to me got it in the stomach," Reed said. "I don't think he made it."

"Someone shot you?" I was incredulous. I wanted to laugh.

"An Israeli sniper." Reed cradled his arm as if it were a badge of honor. "Revolution, brother, the real thing," he said. "Twelve-year-old kids blowing themselves to pieces on Israeli buses. They're committed. You have to admire that."

Reed stood up and walked into the kitchen, raising his voice so I could hear. "Oppression. That's what it is." He returned with a full glass of tamarind nectar. "Bullies," he went on, staring down at the glass as if reading something in its dark surface. He walked to the window. "Isn't the world full of bullies, from the playground to the corporate office to the White House? Aren't they everywhere?"

"Everywhere," I said, not in agreement or denial, but merely because that's what Reed wanted to hear. His breath came in short bursts. I looked at my watch and wondered if my parents were in bed yet.

Reed paced the room, passing the glass from one hand to the other. "When I was in Venice last summer, I ran into Liz Schuller at a bar near San Marco's Square. What were the chances, right? You remember Liz from high school? Carly Cantwell's best friend. You remember Carly. Your little crush."

"Carly Cantwell," I said, her name strange on my tongue. We'd had some classes together our junior and senior years. We'd studied together a few times. She was a shy girl, a state champion swimmer with curly blonde hair and a lean body tempered through long hours of cutting through water. I had a crush on her, sure, one of those pubescent musings that never comes to anything. She wanted to be a doctor, I remembered. I wondered about her sometimes when searching my bookcase and seeing the green and gold binding of my high school yearbook. "Did Liz mention Carly?" I asked.

"Oh, yeah, buddy, she mentioned Carly," Reed said. "In fact, I think she told me a little more than she wanted to. *In vino veritas*, if you know what I mean."

"What'd she say?" I tried to sound casual but suddenly found it difficult to breathe. I wondered if something had happened to Carly.

Reed stopped his pacing and looked at me. "You really want to know? You ready for this? Denny Bradshaw raped her the summer after our senior year. It happened at a house party up on Lea Hill. He cornered her in a bedroom. Sure, she tried to fight him off tooth and nail, but Denny's huge. And in the middle of it some girl walks in and then just turns around and leaves. Doesn't do a damn thing. Carly's crying for help and the girl bolts."

I stared at my hands. They suddenly felt cold. "Did she tell the police?" I asked. I wanted to hear that justice had been done, that Denny had been punished, though I already knew the answer.

Reed sat on the coffee table and leaned in toward me. "You see, that's the kicker, my friend. Right as Denny's zipping up, he tells Carly he'll kill her if she ever tells. She's in shock for about a week before Liz convinces her to report what happened. But the police won't do a thing. That's the legal system for you. They'll give you all the justice you want unless it interferes with what Big Daddy Bradshaw's passing under the table."

Denny Bradshaw was a grade above us, a high school athlete whose father sat on the school board and owned the largest construction company in Auburn. I remembered Denny as the arrogant jock with his shoulder lowered, pushing through the school hallways as if moving down the field, shouting at anyone in his way. At least once a week at lunch he'd stop at our table with a couple of jock friends, wave a hamburger in our faces and laugh hysterically. Once he overturned a garbage can on top of our heads. After high school, he went to Washington State on a football scholarship but lasted only a couple of years before dropping out and moving back to Auburn to work in the family business. I'd heard a rumor that his father cut him off for embezzling money.

"And you know the girl who walks in on this," Reed said, "the only witness who can put Denny away? She's a secretary at Bradshaw Construction, started a few weeks after the rape. A real coincidence. And what about all the other victims? Liz said there were always rumors."

"It's not right," I said. I looked down at my fisted hands.

"Of course it's not right. It's a travesty." Reed walked to the window and glowered at the darkness beyond the glass. "And with guys like Denny the great injustice is that it keeps happening. I'd bet my life on it. Seven years after high school, you think he's changed? The man's a predator and we're going to stop him."

Reed turned and stared at me, as if expecting me to say something.

"What? You want to blindside him in an alley?" I asked. "Sneak up behind him with a tire iron? Is that what you're suggesting?"

"Hell no," Reed said. "I'd never harm a living thing. That's not what I do. I want to shame him. I was thinking about a little body work on his car, leave a message he'll understand, let him know somebody's watching."

"Reed, come on." I tried to laugh. "This is crazy. Really."

"I've done some reconnaissance," Reed said. "He works at that old bar on Main Street. The Mecca. He parks in the back. One or two minutes. In and out. We'll leave him a nice note."

"I'm in law school," I said. "We get caught and I'm ruined. I couldn't take the bar."

"Is that all you care about now?" Reed asked. "Come on. If we don't do it, then who will?"

"It just doesn't feel right," I said.

Reed laughed. "Doesn't feel right? Isn't there a higher law? The spirit of the law? Don't you believe that? And what about everything we used to believe in? Making the world a better place. Helping those who can't help themselves. Don't you believe that anymore?" Reed ran his thumb over the short stubble on his chin. "Okay, think about it this way: what about that rapist running wild out there? Does that feel right? What about some justice for Carly? Doesn't she deserve it?" When I didn't say anything, Reed kept talking. "Don't you see this shit every day on the news? The Denny Bradshaws of the world pushing their way through life, knocking people to the ground, mouthing off, wanting a free ride? Don't you remember how he'd push us around? And let me ask you this. Didn't it always piss you off that we couldn't do a damn thing about it? But what if we could? Tell me, Derrick, and be honest, how would it feel to stick it to Denny? To send him a message?"

I didn't say anything, just stared at my hands, but I knew it would be wonderful, sheer bliss.

"You want to do what's right by the law," Reed said. "I respect that. I value that. But I'm going."

Two weeks later Reed called me in Provo.

"Man, it was just like old times," he said, "fighting injustice and oppression." Reed's voice sounded as if it were percolating up from the bottom of the ocean. "Hey, I'm in El Salvador until June and then it's off to Honduras. Maybe you've already heard about the exploitation down here, about the sweatshops. Nike, Reebok, Gap. We're talking nineteenth-century England, children working their fingers to nubs for a dollar a day. So how about it?"

I felt the weight of the phone on my shoulder, and then the heat building between my ear and the molded plastic.

"Correct me if I'm wrong," Reed said, "but maybe you're not interested."

I moved the phone to my other ear.

"I hope," Reed continued, "that you don't hold something against me."

"No, it's not that," I said, and then I thought: *It's what you are and what I am now. I don't want to be you. I can't be you.* I remembered Denny's car, not the souped-up muscle car I'd expected, but a beige sedan, clean and well maintained, the kind of car my dad would buy. A small photograph in a plastic frame hung from the rearview mirror: a woman in a white dress holding a baby, and behind her lush trees and lawn.

There was a momentary roar on the other end of the line—a passing truck or bus. I imagined the tropical heat, the crowds of dark, perspiring bodies, the chatter of a language I didn't understand, the foulness of rotting garbage.

"Derrick, I know what you're thinking," Reed said. "You're thinking, 'He made me do it. He made me smash that car. The sinner made me sin.' Have you become one of them, Derrick? You gonna say your prayers tonight and write your tithing check Sunday and feel justified because God will right every wrong in the life to come? If you believe that, then you're a bigger sinner than I am."

I unplugged the phone and walked to my bedroom. It was snowing outside, white flakes collecting on the bare branches and dead, yellow lawns. A car passed. The apartment was silent, my roommate gone, shopping or studying in the law library.

From the closet's top shelf I took down a cardboard box full of Reed's letters. Each envelope was decorated with a dizzying arrangement of intricate designs: arabesques, paisleys, loopy-loops twisting and falling in on themselves in a practically untraceable pattern. I saw in the elaborate patterns a complex network of roots going back through the years, back to someone I didn't want to be or think about, back to Reed.

For the next half hour I fed the letters into the shredder under my desk, consoled by the high-pitched whine as the paper disappeared into the machine. I found myself repeating something I'd once read, perhaps something I'd taught in Rio's crumbling *favelas: To rid our lives of sin, we must destroy its roots.*

I never imagined Reed living a long life. He didn't either. In high school, he enjoyed mulling over the possible scenarios of his passing. They were all heroic and horribly violent: pulverized by an explosive harpoon as he protected whales in the northern Atlantic; the human shield ground to a bloody pulp beneath an Israeli tank; hacked to pieces by a crazed band of Islamic militants as they overran a Red Cross hospital in Sudan. For Reed, anything less would have been unworthy of his life, and so he had lived, always searching out that dangerous, altruistic cause to martyr himself for.

So when I answered the phone one Saturday morning and heard my dad's voice—strained, fighting for composure—I knew what he'd say.

"Bob and Edna Swenson called this morning," he said. "It's Reed. He's dead."

I stood in the living room and watched Cassie at the kitchen table, laptop open, searching online for the best stroller and crib money could buy. We'd been married about a year and owned a house in Burbank's Magnolia Park. I was an associate in Latham and Watkins' Los Angeles office.

My dad said the American Embassy in Honduras didn't tell Bob and Edna much, just that Reed was there with a human rights group to protest the treatment of workers at a textile mill outside

Tegucigalpa: picket lines, boycotts, even sabotage of some of the looms. The Honduran police didn't know if Reed's death and the protests were connected, but they found him, stabbed three times in the chest, a block from his hostel, pockets emptied, shoes stolen.

"Do they know anything else?" I asked.

"His knuckles were bruised," my dad said. "He didn't go down easily." And that's what I wanted to hear, that Reed went out fighting.

And then my dad said: "Bob and Edna asked if you'd speak at the funeral. Will you do that? It would mean a lot to them."

Outside, birds chortled in our lemon tree. Down the street someone gunned an engine. "Sure," I said.

I put the phone down and walked to the window. Parked in the driveway, my silver BMW glowed in the mid-morning sun. Cassie's yellow tea roses and Santa Barbara daisies edged the front yard. Later our gardeners, Miguel and Hector, would come to cut the lawn and hedge the bushes. Like my pioneer ancestors, I'd prospered, cultivated my garden, sanctified materialism. I'd served an honorable mission, pursued education, found gainful employment, married in the temple, paid a generous tithe, would soon be a father. I was second counselor in my ward's bishopric. I should have felt like a success.

"Who was that?" Cassie asked.

I turned to look at her. I could already see the small bump pushing at her waistline. "My dad," I said. "Somebody I knew from high school died. He called to tell me."

"A friend?" Cassie asked.

I lifted my laptop and walked to the couch. I'd never told Cassie about Reed, never mentioned our years in high school, nor had my parents. There was something unspoken between my parents and me, as if we'd agreed that those years had never happened. There were other things I hadn't told Cassie. I hadn't told her that twice a year I was sending a check to Amnesty International and Earth First! I hadn't told her that there were some opinions I didn't share with our church friends.

"Just someone I knew," I said. "My parents want me at the funeral, as a favor to the family."

"Are you all right?" Cassie asked.

"I'm fine," I said. "We weren't close."

I needed to buy a plane ticket, pack a bag. I imagined the funeral, the bright chapel and drab organ music, and of course Reed, laid out in a dark suit and white shirt, hair trimmed—finally the missionary his mother had dreamed of. I'd stand at the pulpit and say something kind and comforting, something about Reed's love for all living things. But I couldn't say everything. Gazing out at all those devout, grieving people who believed Reed's life was a tragedy, how could I say that maybe he'd died a brave man, a rich man, a righteous man?

Great Heights

How about a quick swim?" Carolyn asked, pointing to a lighted swimming pool glimmering through the fence of a large apartment complex on North Temple. Norman smiled and continued to drive.

"I'm serious," Carolyn said. "We did it all the time at BYU. Just walk in like you live there and jump in. It's fun."

Norman didn't feel comfortable sneaking in, treading the chilly water in his Levi's, and then driving home shivering and dripping onto the car seats and floor mats. "You're not in college anymore," he wanted to say. "What if we get caught? It's against the law." Instead he said, "It's late."

Carolyn stared at him, her pink lip gloss sparkling in the dim light. "Norman, you can be a real stick-in-the-mud," she said.

Though Norman didn't tell her, the comment angered him.

The next evening Norman got a call from Cameron, an old friend who now lived in Salt Lake City with his wife, Erica, not far from Norman's apartment in West Valley.

Cameron and Norman had grown up together outside Seattle and had been roommates at BYU before their missions. A year ago, out of the blue, Cameron had suddenly taken an interest in Norman's social life, even setting Norman up with a few interns from the law firm where he worked. Norman hadn't liked any of them. And then when Norman began dating Carolyn, Cameron called weekly to pump him for information.

"So what's the deal?" Cameron asked. "Getting serious? Should I make room in my busy schedule for your wedding? I'm joking. No pressure, really."

"I like Carolyn," Norman said. "It's just that we have different ideas of what's fun." He told Cameron about the night before, about the swimming pool and Carolyn's jab about being a stick-in-the-mud. "Sometimes I wonder about her judgment," Norman said. "I mean, you can get in big trouble for doing that. It's trespassing."

"Lighten up," Cameron said. "Isn't that what I'm always saying? The poor girl just wanted to have some fun, live a little." There was a burst of static over the line. "So that's your big hang-up, different ideas of what's fun?"

"It's not just that," Norman said. "I know it's silly. I shouldn't even mention it." He cleared his throat. "She leaves food out. Perishables like cheese and milk. And she doesn't hang her clothes up. She just tosses them over her dresser until they're this huge mound. And she's always losing her keys."

"Cheese and milk and keys? You're joking," Cameron said. "Come on, Norman. Be serious. Tell me you're joking, so I don't think you're a head case."

"It's an indicator," Norman said. "I'm not saying it's a showstopper, but she has issues we'll have to work out."

"A little spoiled milk and you're ready to dump her," Cameron said. "Aren't you being a little unfair? As a high school guidance counselor, wouldn't you agree?"

"They're bad habits," Norman said.

"You're thirty years old," Cameron said, "and you can't stop thinking about the spoiled milk and the pile of clothes. Remember how you stayed with us while you were looking for an apartment? It took you two months. Every place had something you didn't like, roommates too loud or too messy, too far from work, too small. Then you end up renting your own place because you couldn't stand living with anyone. You know what happens to guys who can't stop thinking about the spoiled milk and the pile of clothes? They live alone because no one can stand them. You see what I mean, Norman? I wash my hands of you." Then he shouted into the phone: "I'm sorry. I didn't mean that. I'll call you next week."

Norman sat on the couch, the phone still cradled between his cheek and shoulder, pondering the sliver of moon outside the window and the white, wispy clouds shooting past it. Privately, he valued little of what Cameron said. He remembered Cameron as a floppy-haired, gangly teenager dabbing his wet nose and weepy eyes with his shirtsleeve after confessing to Bishop Belnap that he'd felt up Tiffany Orton in the high school parking lot after a football game. He remembered when Cameron and Erica were dating, how she berated Cameron in front of his friends, snapping her fingers to get his attention. Who's Cameron to give relationship advice? Norman thought. He'd married a piece of work, a bland, materialistic gossip who racked up a mountain of debt, a downer who scowled at Norman and sighed loudly whenever he spoke. At least I won't make the same mistakes, Norman thought, and the truth of those words comforted him.

Norman continued to date Carolyn. There were dinners at the Old Spaghetti Factory and Buca di Beppo's, Saturday matinees in Sugarhouse, hiking Millcreek or Big Cottonwood Canyon. When Carolyn's parents visited from California, Norman met them. Over dinner at Biaggi's, he formed the opinion that both were sensible people, unobtrusive but caring, moderate in the car they drove and the clothes they wore. Financially, they were secure; physically and mentally, there appeared to be nothing out of the ordinary. In fact, Norman was impressed with Carolyn's mother's physique. At forty-seven she still ran the Santa Barbara marathon every year. If it's true that the daughter becomes the mother, then Norman would be satisfied with what Carolyn would become.

Their relationship was predictable, no surprises. Maybe I love Carolyn, Norman thought. Maybe. But he couldn't let go the memory of her sitting in the dimly lit car, arms folded, her lip gloss sparkling: *Norman, you can be a real stick-in-the-mud.* There were other images that bothered him: a chest of drawers piled with clothes, a forgotten gallon of milk warming on the countertop, Carolyn rifling through the couch cushions to find her keys.

Then in the beginning of June, Carolyn told Norman that she was moving home for the summer. This revelation was so sudden that Norman, upon hearing her announcement, began reviewing the past few weeks, the past few months, searching for any premonition of her decision. He'd suspected something earlier that afternoon when Carolyn had called to tell him they needed to talk.

"My roommate's sister said she'd take over my lease for the summer," Carolyn told Norman that evening in his apartment. "And I don't begin teaching until the end of August, so why not move home and save a little money? My brother's home from his mission in a couple of weeks. My family hasn't been together in two years. It is sudden, I know." She sat solemnly on Norman's couch, hugging a cushion to her chest. She wore a black, short-sleeved turtleneck sweater, cashmere or merino wool, with a raised pattern of lines on its front. Norman wondered how much it had cost and why she hadn't told him about buying it.

"It's sudden," he said.

In the stairwell a dog barked, a hoarse discharge amplified by the concrete walls and steps. Carolyn leaned forward, squinting into the night beyond the window, and Norman, sitting on an ottoman in front of her, thought he saw in her sunken shoulders and narrow eyes a shudder of emotion, until he realized she was squinting to read the titles on the bookshelf near the window.

"I don't want you to feel," Carolyn said, "that you can't see other people. We'll keep in touch. It's for the best. Don't you think?"

A buzzing filled the room: the faint electrical whir of Norman's laptop on the side table, the overhead fluorescent lights, a moth batting against the window. Carolyn's voice, blanched of emotion, seemed lost in the room's sterile banality.

Norman traced the faux wood grain in the coffee table with his finger, taking in this new information. He was shocked, not at Carolyn's summer plan, but at how quickly and dispassionately she was dispatching him. All evening she'd hardly looked at him, but not out of embarrassment or uneasiness. She was already gone, already sunning herself on Huntington Beach, already a thousand miles away. This tidy tapering of their relationship into nothing, was just another errand for her today, he felt, another checked box on a list under *change oil* and *pay phone bill.*

"I can't help think that I've done something wrong," Norman said. "If I did, I hope you'd tell me."

"No, it's not like that," Carolyn said. "I'm not angry." She let her hands fall to her thighs. "I never told you this, but before we started dating, I'd just ended a relationship with a guy from my old ward. He taught snowboarding in Park City. He was twenty, wasn't thinking about a mission, had never been to college, didn't think about anything, really, except snowboarding. His life was this chaotic mess that sucked me in. He never had enough money to pay his bills. He was always doing these stupid things to scare me: driving too fast, rock climbing without a rope, hiding behind doors and jumping out. That's why I liked you. You were different. You were cautious. You made me feel safe." She tugged pensively at a strand of hair that had fallen into her face. "You've been great, and I've had some fun, but you're too cautious. Maybe this doesn't make any sense. It's like you don't leave anything to chance. It's like you're always looking down at everything around you from some great height, weighing options, qualifying, planning your next move. Sometimes I feel you see everything as if it were an algebra problem and you're solving for X, even with me, trying to see if I add up. You can't categorize everything. Not everything adds up, even when it's right."

Suddenly Norman felt angry, the same anger he'd felt after Carolyn's dig in the car. "What's wrong with caution?" he demanded, slamming his palm down on the coffee table. An unlit red candle at the table's center teetered in its black terra-cotta saucer, then toppled over. Carolyn looked at him with wide, shocked eyes.

"I get sick of hearing about how recklessness is this endearing quality"—Norman made a deliberate effort to lower his voice—"the rebellious charm girls love." His hands shook. He glared at Carolyn, feeling a certain pleasure in now having her full attention. "What kind of world is it where people get by on dumb luck and good graces? Not a world I want any part of."

He tried to explain, how he remembered the inattentive, bored faces of some of his high school classmates: Andy Dumas, Jimmy Richards, Danny Manetas. He could name others. They'd done poorly, spent their money on stereo equipment and custom rims for their cars, smoked weed in the school parking lot, boozed it up, and bedded any girl they could. They strutted across campus, blithe grins smeared across their faces, heads thrown back, squinting through black shades, with not a care in the world, sporting a reckless, live-for-today charm that the girls, and even the teachers, found endearing. Watching them, Norman had experienced a nascent pleasure he couldn't articulate then, knowing they'd reached their zenith, that for them life after high school would be a tedious struggle, an existence made up of depleting habits and regrets, of forever trying to recapture a freedom they'd never really had. How could Norman make Carolyn understand? Caution, vigilance, planning. These were a safeguard against catastrophe. These were the secrets of success.

"I can't live in that world," Carolyn said. "I can't live in a place where it's always me against everybody else, where I'm constantly on guard, trying to anticipate what's next." She stood and walked to the door, pausing there, one hand resting on the knob, the other fisted on her hip. "I don't even want to ask what you really think about me, Norman. I'm only beginning to see all the ways I don't measure up. I'm starting to wonder why you even asked me out in the first place. Seeing you now in your high, moral tower, I'm wondering how you can ask anyone out."

The door closed with a sharp snap. Norman stood, as if to follow Carolyn, but then sat down.

For the rest of the evening, Norman tried to read through a *Newsweek* article about a school shooting in Ohio, but he understood very little of it. The words floated on the page so that he had to reread sentences and whole paragraphs. Finally, he closed the magazine and lay on the couch, replaying the argument with Carolyn and picking through it, rehearsing what he might have said. For a moment, this image—the image of him bounding down the concrete steps toward the parking lot, putting his arm around Carolyn's shoulders as he asserted his defense—satisfied him. But it quickly soured as he thought of himself standing before her, solidifying the very image of himself that she disliked.

At 10:00 p.m., not fully understanding why, Norman searched the Internet for the names and addresses of jewelers in Salt Lake.

Norman picked up the ring on Saturday.

Excited and carefree, he drove up Little Cottonwood Canyon, cracking the window to let the cool air wash over him. He wanted to speak with someone, to pull the polished ring case from his pocket and confess his plan to drive to California to propose to Carolyn. Calling his parents wasn't an option. Norman knew his father would tell him he was acting impulsively, and he feared his father's concern about the cost of the ring.

Norman couldn't think of anyone from his ward to share in his excitement. Plus, news of his impending journey and intentions might reach Carolyn before his arrival. In the end, Norman drove to Cameron's house.

"Who's there?" Erica asked after Norman knocked at the door. He told her and then heard a profanity and a slamming cupboard door.

Cameron opened the door, squinting through the radiant morning light. "It's early."

"It's almost eleven," Norman said.

"We were up late," Cameron said. He stepped out of the doorway to let Norman pass. "Hurry up before I change my mind."

The living room was still dark and shaded, but Norman could see the clutter from last night's festivities: the coffee table crowded with empty soda cans, pizza boxes, and a Monopoly board. Erica, in a blue terrycloth robe, loafed on a naugahyde couch the color of peanut butter, and Cameron paced the room, tidying things up, chatting nervously.

"New couch?" Norman asked.

"I guess we haven't seen you in a while," Cameron said, sweeping the Monopoly pieces and paper money into the box with his palm. "And check out the 60-inch flatscreen."

"How much that set you back?"

"About two grand."

Norman made a sucking noise. "Two grand," he repeated, throwing a quick glance at Erica. Her silence was unnerving. She stared at him, head slightly tipped forward, scrutinizing him from where she sat.

"Well, unlike you," Cameron said, "We're not in a monastic order. We actually spend our money."

Still standing near the door, unsure of what do with his hands, Norman wondered why Cameron hadn't asked him to sit down.

"So what about you?" asked Cameron. "Still dating that girl? What's her name? Carrie, right?"

"Carolyn," Norman said, "and funny you ask. We're getting married. Or at least I plan to ask her."

"That poor girl," Erica said, breaking her bored silence. She thumbed through a *Cosmopolitan* and yawned.

"She's always so sarcastic in the morning," Cameron said, shooting Erica a look that Norman couldn't interpret. "You know how she is. She never wakes up until noon."

"This will wake her up." Norman pulled the ring case from his pant pocket and opened it. Even in the room's weak light, the diamonds sparkled.

Erica perked up, rising slightly onto her knee to examine the ring.

"Cubic zirconium and white gold," Erica said. "Or is it sterling silver? I know you, Norman. You wouldn't spend more than a few hundred dollars."

"Platinum setting and a one carat diamond," Norman said. "Eight thousand dollars plus tax and insurance. Monday I drive to California. Ring. Flowers. Down on one knee. Right in front of her family."

"Where's that old Norman Reeves?" Cameron said, grinning. "So unlike you. This from the guy who wouldn't go to our senior class party because he'd be out too late."

"Does it have a return policy?" Erica asked flatly.

"Ignore her," Cameron said. "We're both happy for you. We really are. Aren't we, honey?" Cameron moved toward the door and Norman followed. "Taking the plunge and all, that's great, really great. Your mother will be happy. Somebody to clutter your life a little. That'll be good for you." He pointed at his watch. "I don't mean to hurry you along, but I have some work friends coming over to watch the Dodgers game and we need to scour this place." He opened the door.

"I'll send an announcement," Norman said.

"You do that," Cameron said.

Norman wanted to ask if someone in a monastic order would plop down eight grand for a ring, but the door closed before he could. As he walked to his car, Norman wondered why Cameron hadn't asked him to stay and watch the game.

Eighty miles into Nevada, a translucent veil of acrid, yellowish smoke began pouring from beneath Norman's car. There was a sharp metallic sound, and then the car stalled, lurching to a stop on the shoulder. Norman turned the key, but the engine wouldn't start. Tracing the faint line of Interstate 80 on his worn atlas, Norman had only a vague memory of the town he'd just passed: a casino with a flashing billboard, a gas station, a decaying mobile home park surrounded by a sagging chain-link fence. Wells, Nevada.

Norman tried to get his bearings. Not far off the road, he saw a dilapidated ranch house, almost lost in the blanched landscape. He considered walking there to ask for help, but then out of the dusty heat a kid in a green pickup, wearing a frayed cowboy hat and no shirt, pulled over and offered to send a tow truck. Norman thanked him and waited by the car, lifting his head and squinting into the fierce sun whenever a vehicle topped the rise on the interstate and agitated the desert's vast, ghostly silence.

After forty-five minutes a tow truck materialized through the waves of blurry heat rising off the highway—a massive vehicle with a long flatbed and chrome exhaust pipes on each side of the cab. The tow man nodded as he pulled onto the shoulder and then backed up until the truck's bumper almost touched Norman's car. The tow man jumped from the cab and made a business of putting on a pair of soiled leather gloves, gaping at Norman through dark sunglasses and smirking as if what he saw amused him. Leaning against the cab of the truck, he yanked a lever that sent the bed into a sluggish, grinding tilt, and while waiting, he lifted his glasses and wiped at his forehead with the back of his gloved hand. "I can get you back to town," the tow man said, staring at Norman with dark, bulging eyes. "We got a mechanic there. He'll take care of you."

"How much for the tow?" Norman asked.

"Ain't going to be cheap," the man said. "We're a good twenty-five miles from town."

Wanting to say "I bet it's never cheap," Norman, instead, said nothing, slightly cheered that his MasterCard provided a towing reimbursement for such emergencies.

"I bet you're wondering how I'm going to do this," the tow man said. A big rig bombed past in a great rush of noise and air. The man didn't flinch.

"Pardon," Norman said.

"I bet you're wondering," the man said slowly, making a little pantomime with his gloved hands, one palm rubbing against the other, "how I'm going to get your car on the bed of this here truck." He opened a metal box under the truckbed and pulled out four greasy chains. "Everyone wonders. Last week I had a vanload of Japs stop to take pictures of me loading a car. They took a hundred pictures. I swear to God."

Not knowing what to say, Norman said nothing, relieved when clattering chains and the shrill whine of hydraulics discouraged any conversation. Gazing at the broad sky, Norman fingered the ring case in his front pocket. The sun, suspended in the expansive sky like a child's ball, had reached its apex and made everything look washed-out and muted—dingy browns and dull greens in every direction. Norman kicked at a faded beer can and sent it skidding down the gravel embankment.

The man hooked a chain to the car's undercarriage and slowly hoisted the vehicle up the angled bed. Norman watched the mechanical process, the pulley motor straining, the car inching forward against the tug of gravity, shuddering slightly—a fly suspended in a web. Then the bed of the truck came level, and the tow man secured the chains over the axles and boomed them down. He waved Norman to the passenger door.

Norman lowered his head and climbed into the cab, nudging himself into the mess collecting on the worn vinyl seat: fast-food wrappers, loose papers, and a few glossy magazines with women in bikinis bent provocatively over the hoods and roofs of flashy, souped-up cars. The cab smelled distinctly of motor oil and dirt, and the air was thick with dust. Norman rifled through the clutter around him searching for the seat belt latch, ready to plunge his hand into the seat's dark crevice when the tow man spoke:

"Won't find it," he said, slamming the truck into gear, spinning the tires as he pulled onto the road. "Got rid of them a while ago. Read something once about how many people die from wearing seat belts. Car rolls into a lake, you can't get your seat belt off. It happens more than you think. Know what I mean?"

Norman made a low grunting noise. He wanted to collapse into himself, empty his lungs of air and be gone, close his eyes and wake up a hundred miles from this stifling cab and the crass figure occupying its foul space.

"My friends call me Curly," the tow man said, extending a callused hand that Norman reluctantly grasped. Curly's forearms were thick and tanned, the muscles like tight rope pushing against the skin, and Norman couldn't help thinking how pale and soft his hand was in Curly's sturdy grip.

Curly wore a gun on his hip, partly concealed under the stained, threadbare shirt he wore untucked. And when he saw Norman eyeing it, Curly said it was for protection. "Last month alone," he said, "two of my buddies in Elko almost got robbed. The cops call it attempted robbery, but you never know what'll happen. A few years ago, I heard of this tow truck driver out of Vegas. Shot in the head, murdered for forty bucks and then dumped in a ditch. Ask me, I'd say it's these Mexicans moving their drugs across the border. I can see you're a Utah boy by your license plate, and I know you're getting them over there, too. I have an uncle outside St. George. Says you can't pull into Home Depot without almost running one down in the parking lot. Hell, it's the same all over I hear: L.A., Vegas, Salt Lake. And it's not just the drugs and the crime. White people are becoming a minority. Excuse me if that sounds racist, but it keeps me up at night. I have two daughters in Elko. I have to think about them. My family goes back in this county two hundred and fifty years, and some dark-skinned invader from the south waltzes in here and wants a free slice of the pie, wants to take food from my babies' mouths. Don't that piss you off?"

The question bothered Norman, the man bothered Norman, everything within the grasp of Norman's senses bothered him: the abrasive sun, the stifling heat, the dashboard clock flashing the wrong time, Curly's provincial drawl and crude demeanor. Norman had already conceived his own hard-nosed views on illegal immigration, views not so different from Curly's, but he didn't want to concur. He didn't want Curly to think they had anything in common. "It's a complicated issue," Norman said.

"Don't think I'm racist," Curly said. "Not at all. But some of these people will steal your car because they think you're the rich white guy. They don't care about giving, they just want to take, and they don't care from who. And then you see it on the news, the violence. They'll shoot you in the head and not blink an eye. They're monsters." Curly adjusted the air vent and cleared his throat. "Hope I haven't offended you. But you have to understand my work: dark, deserted roads, strangers. I'll admit it: I'm one who hears things in the dark."

He smiled. Norman could see his yellow teeth. "Hell, I wish all my customers were like you, clean-cut white bread. You know, you look like a guy I knew in high school, this guy voted Nicest in Class. No joking. Scott Chandler, great guy. You could have nailed his sister to a tree and skinned her alive, and he wouldn't have raised his voice. No one liked him, though. Too nice. Boring."

Curly, as if suddenly taking notice of the filth surrounding him, threw a few of the magazines and some of the hamburger wrappers behind the seat. "So tell me," he said, "a good boy like you, what's the worst thing you ever did?"

The heat and the cadenced hum of the diesel engine had lulled Norman into semiconsciousness. He'd listened to little of what Curly had said, but the question jolted Norman awake.

Curly smiled, showing his dingy teeth and gray, swollen gums. "The worst thing you've ever done. Just between me and you. Our little secret. The worst thing you never told anyone."

Norman, not knowing why, suddenly felt panic.

"Forget it," Curly said. "Forget I asked." He adjusted the volume on the CB radio near the gearshift.

Norman wiped his damp forehead. The question persisted like a noxious, lingering odor. What was the worst thing he'd done? On a Webelos campout twenty years ago, he'd tested the blade of his pocketknife on the rainfly of Brother Seegmiller's tent and then blamed Cliff Wallace, a smelly welfare case all the boys called Pigpen.

In junior high, on a dare, he phoned Christie Reed's house when she was at the movies with friends and told her parents she'd been in a car accident. Later, in high school, he and Cameron left an unkind note on the windshield of an obnoxious, overweight girl in their AP European History class. Norman heard she committed suicide a few years after graduation.

Sometimes when he thought about those past cruelties, even after so many years, Norman felt a crippling guilt that subsided only when he repeated to himself, as if it were a mantra, that these mistakes had saved him from larger mistakes. He didn't want to feel more guilt, so he had lived believing that life could quickly turn tragic, one small mistake begetting another, and then another, until something catastrophic and unspeakable occurred. Yet at times, Norman wondered if, in his effort to live his Mormon faith unwaveringly, he'd missed out on something.

The CB crackled. A distant, twangy voice announced the details of a grisly car accident south of town: rollover, station wagon, Lifeflight chopper en route, clean-up requested. Curly whooped loudly. Wide-eyed, licking his lips, he turned to Norman: "That's a hundred and twenty dollars in my pocket."

THREE GUYS AND A GAL AUTOMOTIVE. The faded sign rose above a cinder block building with two open bays gaping like dark, toothless mouths. Dust-stained and deteriorating, the building blended with the barren desert around it. Norman, at first, thought it might be a wrecking yard littered with rows of afflicted cars with flat tires, peeling paint, and gutted interiors.

Curly swung the truck through the chain-link gate and braked harder than was necessary, then jumped from the cab to loosen the chains mooring the car to the truckbed.

"Help me give her a shove," Curly said to Norman, and together they pushed the car into an open bay.

After Curly had returned his credit card, Norman thanked him and walked toward the mechanic's office. Before he reached the door, though, someone called his name. Norman turned and saw Curly jump from the truck and run over. "Listen," he said, panting from the short sprint. "I've been thinking I offended you."

Raising his eyebrows to convey a surprise he didn't feel, Norman said, "No, not at all." And then: "It's been a long day. I just didn't feel like talking much. That's all." Norman, standing in the wash of Curly's rank breath, wondered what this man wanted. Some kind of validation of his worth as a human being? A friendly, sympathetic sounding board? What? A service had been rendered and paid for, a receipt given. Norman thanked Curly again and turned toward the office, feeling he owed this man nothing more.

"I can tell you don't think much of me. Maybe you think I'm some kind of redneck," Curly said, patting the gun on his hip. "Understand, this ain't Utah. This place is out in the middle of nowhere. You see strange things. And this business of making money from accidents"—he looked off toward the interstate and then back to Norman—"it's not like I'm a vulture. Somebody has to do it. Somebody has to get their hands dirty to clean things up. Hell, it puts bread on the table for my babies. Don't that make it all right?"

Norman didn't like Curly's insinuation that because he lived in Utah he was innocent and needed a lecture on the world's sad realities. "Really, I'm not offended," Norman said. "It's just been a long day. I'm tired."

"I get you," Curly said. "I just don't want you to have the wrong impression. You're a nice guy. I thought I might have said something."

Stepping toward the mechanic's office, Norman said, "I'm fine."

"Hey, I'll tell you what," Curly said. "I'll do this job then take you out for a drink, show you the town."

Norman felt his jaw drop, felt the dry wind on the tip of his tongue. He looked up and down the narrow street, Wells's main thoroughfare. To the west he could see the blinking lights of the casino billboard and to the east a few bars and a mobile home park. "I appreciate the offer," Norman said, "but I'll be back on the road by then."

"On the road?" Curly said. "You're not going anywhere today. That engine's toast. I can smell it from here. So what do you say? My treat."

"I don't drink," Norman said.

"Then a cup of coffee."

"I don't drink coffee."

"That's right. You're one of those Mormon boys," Curly said.

"You wear a short leash. I respect that. How about a soda? You drink soda?"

Norman couldn't speak. He knew Curly wouldn't take no for an answer. "All right. A soda."

"Good," Curly said. "About two hours. I'll be back." He mounted the truck and, just before closing the door, said: "Hey, tonight you can even crash at my place if you want."

Norman watched the truck move toward the freeway and knew he'd make sure to be somewhere else when Curly returned.

Norman sat on an old, sun-bleached couch in the mechanic's office and read a yellowed newspaper he found between the couch cushions. Through an open door that led to the garage, he watched the two mechanics. Both wore navy-blue coveralls unzipped to the waist, exposing their hairy, distended bellies. One smoked a cigarette near the open bay door, and the other was bent over the engine of a black Ford truck, tapping his heavy black boots to a radio blaring "Crazy Train." Norman's car, its hood up, sat forlornly on the far end of garage. Norman looked at his watch and drew a long breath.

"Gee, I hope you don't need to be somewhere," a woman said. She walked across the room and sat at a metal desk cluttered with yellow carbon copies and coffee mugs smudged with oily fingerprints. She grabbed a bag of potato chips on the desk and started eating. She was about Norman's age, tan skin, blond.

"No hope of getting out today?" Norman said, hoping his expectant smile might prompt her to hurry the mechanics.

"I'll be honest," she said. "This is the only garage in town. These guys don't hurry." She tipped the bag of chips in Norman's direction. "Want some?"

"No, thanks," Norman said.

"It's probably for the best," she said, throwing the bag on the desk. "Doctors say these things will kill you. Hydrogenated oil. That's what does it."

"Bad stuff," Norman said. He peered through the dusty window at the sign. Its shadow now touched the end of the parking lot.

"I'm the gal," the woman said.

Norman turned from the window. "Pardon me?"

She pointed to the sign. "Three Guys and a Gal. I'm the gal."

She crossed her legs and smiled, showing a row of straight teeth so white it seemed that light emanated from them. Norman wanted to compliment her teeth but decided against it, thinking she might interpret this as a come-on.

Through the open door came the sound of metal striking concrete. The mechanic working on the black Ford picked up a long wrench that had fallen to the floor and began playing it as if it were a guitar. The other mechanic stood over Norman's car, peering at the engine, the burning nub of a cigarette pinched between his black fingers.

"So you're the gal?" Norman said, cheered at the sight of the mechanic. "Where's the third mechanic? He get fired and nobody changed the sign?"

It was meant as a joke, but the woman didn't smile. "Oh, he's not around anymore," she said. She picked up some papers and stared at them a moment before putting them aside. "I'm Maggie," she said, smiling again.

Norman meant for the conversation to stop there, but Maggie asked him a few questions, and to be polite, he asked her a few. She'd lived in Wells most of her life, except for a couple of years she spent in Colorado. She wasn't married and had worked at the garage for the last three years. "But this isn't the only thing I do," Maggie said. "If this job was the only thing that defined me, I'd go crazy. This is just something steady with benefits, something to pay the bills. What I really like to do is make these herbal products, soaps and oils, facial scrubs, lotions. I sell them online. It's all about helping people achieve balance, about finding inner peace."

"Soaps and oils," Norman said. "I didn't realize there was much of a market."

"Sure," Maggie said. "I've shipped my products as far as New Zealand and Norway. It's all stuff I make at home. There's a personalized touch. People like that."

Norman imagined large bubbling vats and Maggie standing over them in goggles and a rubber apron, pouring in beakers of scented oils. He imagined her body as she stirred the vats, her hips turning in small circles, her bare arms, a glistening line of sweat on her upper lip. He stared at the weave in the brown carpet and ran his hand quickly across his forehead as if to erase this image of Maggie from his mind.

"So what about you?" Maggie asked. "I don't even know your name."

"Norman Reeves."

"Norman Reeves," Maggie said, repeating the name a few times as if practicing it. "I can't say I've met many Normans. In fact, you might be the first. The only Norman I know is Norman Bates from *Psycho*." Maggie narrowed her eyes and lowered her voice to an ominous whisper. "So do you have your dead mother stashed away somewhere? Do you dress in her clothes and speak in her voice and prey on vulnerable young women searching for a new life?"

"Nothing that exciting," Norman said, grasping the joke. "It's a family name. My great-grandfather—I don't know how many greats back—pulled a handcart across the snowy plains to the Salt Lake Valley. I guess the name's supposed to be inspiring. I've never liked it. And the diminutive's worse. Norm. It makes me think of an obese alcoholic."

"What? You think you got problems?" Maggie said. She leaned forward as if to impart a confidence, and Norman could smell her perfume, something like vanilla. "I'll tell you a secret," she whispered. "Maggie's my middle name. I'm really named after my grandma." She looked around and then spoke. "Her name was Elva. Isn't that horrible?"

Laughing, his hand covering his mouth, Norman tried to think of something to say. He felt awkward and disoriented, finding it strange that after all that had happened, he now sat with a beautiful woman, having nothing to say, unsure if he should even be talking to her.

"So what do you do?" Maggie asked. "For work, I mean." And when Norman told her, she said: "It must be nice to help people."

Norman cleared his throat and stared at the faded floral print on the couch. "It is," Norman said.

This admission, that he was a guidance counselor, always got the same response from those who didn't know him: *It must be nice to help people*. This bothered Norman. Those who knew him better, though, always confessed that they'd have pegged him as something else, an accountant or an engineer, someone who worked with numbers, not a high school guidance counselor. Privately, Norman felt he was a poor match for his chosen profession. He thought of the students who passed through his office, most of them slackers, oozing a palpable bravado and indifference he could sense in the way they shuffled along with no hurry or urgency, faces as blank as cue balls, slouching and yawning as he intoned the rhetoric of fear, quoting statistics on drug use, hefting glossy pictures of doe-eyed meth addicts, painting the stark realities of the adult world as vividly as possible. And then there were the more troubled students Norman met with weekly, kids who exuded a deep hatred for everything around them. He sensed they heard nothing but white noise when he spoke, saw nothing but a hypocrite in a shirt and tie reciting facts. Norman often wondered if they saw in him a contempt for the world and a disaffection equal to their own, a pained, lonely cynic as broken and jaded as themselves.

Norman's scalp tingled. A dull ache pulsed behind his eyes. The waiting room was too hot. Who was he to lecture anyone? Who was he to speak with authority? He couldn't even get to California. He couldn't even keep a girlfriend.

"I don't have any formal training, but I think I know when people need help," Maggie said. "Like when I walked in here. I saw you were having a bad day. Maybe sometimes it's enough just to talk with someone, to have a connection, and that makes a problem seem smaller. That's the way I see things. Is that strange?"

"Not at all," Norman said. He could truthfully say he felt better just talking with Maggie.

She rubbed her right knee and then straightened both legs. "So where you going?"

"California," Norman said. And then he told Maggie about Carolyn, about the ring in his pocket and his plan to propose.

"Very romantic," Maggie said. "And she doesn't know you're coming?"

"No idea at all," Norman said.

At that moment one of the mechanics walked into the office. Norman jumped, suddenly panicked, as if he'd been caught doing something wrong.

"Don't you need to deposit those checks?" the man asked Maggie.

She pulled an envelope from the top desk drawer and said:

"I almost forgot." She looked over her shoulder as she walked through the door. "It's been nice talking to you, Norman."

"It has," Norman said, noticing she had the smallest limp, a favoring of the left leg over the right. She got in a blue pickup truck and drove toward the interstate.

"Women," the mechanic said, sitting down heavily behind the desk. "Especially this one. She's a dreamer, head in the clouds, always talking about the stars and the moon." He yawned and scratched at a wiry tuft of dark hair poking through the neck of his coveralls.

Norman cleared his throat. "My car?"

The mechanic pulled a short section of black rubber hose from his pocket and flopped it on the desk. "You see that hole? You lost all your radiator fluid. Overheated and shot your engine to hell. Blown head gasket."

Norman knew very little about cars, but had a vague notion that a blown head gasket was a major problem. "How much?" he asked.

"How much?" the mechanic said. "That's what everyone wants to know." He took a thick green book from a shelf above the desk, began flipping through the pages and then writing columns of numbers on a legal pad. "Parts and labor will cost two thousand," he said, "plus or minus a hundred. I might have to replace the water pump."

The words were like a kick to the guts. Norman, speechless, stared at the mechanic's name embroidered on his coveralls. *Lou.* The name was like a stereotype, like a joke people make about bad mechanics.

"So what do you want to do?" the mechanic asked. He'd found the bag of potato chips and shoved a handful in his mouth.

"Are you sure?" Norman said. "That seems high."

"Positive," the mechanic said. "It's straight from the book. Look for yourself." He smiled. "I'd tell you to get a second opinion, but what can you do?"

Norman knew the cost of repairs wasn't worth it. The car had been his grandmother's, her gift when he graduated from college. He could get another car. What bothered him was that he wanted out of this town. He looked around the office, at the faded walls and furniture, all in various stages of decay, just like the town. People live here. The thought baffled Norman.

By now the mechanic was drumming his fingers against the cover of the green book, waiting.

"I don't even think the car's worth two thousand dollars," Norman said.

"I got a buddy who owns a junkyard across town," the mechanic said. "He'll probably give you fifty bucks for it." He picked at the grit under his thumbnail with the tip of a pencil. "I still have to charge you a twenty-five dollar diagnostic fee."

Norman handed the cash over. The mechanic counted the bills and then shoved them in his pocket. "I don't mean to hurry you along," he said, standing up, "but we're closing. If you want, there's a motel near the freeway, about a ten minute walk. I think a Greyhound bus passes by there tomorrow afternoon or maybe the day after tomorrow."

A hot wind blew through the empty streets. Overhead the streetlights flickered and made an annoying buzzing sound. Norman, a backpack with a few clothes and toiletries slung over his shoulder, walked toward a restaurant he'd seen earlier from Curly's truck, a stucco building with a neon sign broadcasting its name in an obnoxious red. Norman would call Cameron for a ride and then have dinner while he waited.

The restaurant was locked, though Norman could hear voices inside. He pressed a button next to the door and waited. A woman in a low-cut red dress and black stiletto heels, blonde and heavily made-up, opened the door. "What can I do for you?" she said in a low, breathy voice. She stared at Norman, her lips constricted, as if she were suppressing laughter.

"Is there a phone I can use?" Norman asked.

"Come in," she said, leaning against the doorjamb, giving Norman barely enough room to squeeze by. "Just the phone? That's it?" She spoke the words slowly.

"I might order something, too," Norman said, feeling her soft breasts touch his shoulder as he slid past. She smelled of lavender, an overpowering scent Norman could taste in the back of his throat. "Is there a menu?"

The playfulness drained from the woman's face. "A menu? You're serious?"

"Isn't this a restaurant?" Norman asked.

The woman laughed. "Honey, you got the wrong place. I bet you thought I was your waitress, didn't you? Thought I'd walk you to a table and take your order."

Norman could feel the crimson burning in his cheeks, could see the rising color in his cheeks reflected in an antique mirror near the door, could see himself crumpling, shoulders falling, arms crossed tightly across his chest.

"You never heard of the Ranch House?" she asked. "Where you from?"

"I just need to make a call," Norman said, looking around the room. "Just the phone."

Men, mostly truckers, Norman thought, from the big rigs in the parking lot, sat around wooden tables, playing cards. And why hadn't Norman noticed? No plates on the tables, no crumpled napkins, no smell of food, only stale cigarette smoke, alcohol, and perfume. The room hummed with a palpable tension, a tightness and anticipation in the men's eager faces, animating their coarse speech. Their eyes darted about, drawn to a pulled black curtain at the back of the room. Norman felt revulsion for all of them. He wanted to run out the door as a sign of protest but knew this woman would laugh at him. He'd be the amusing story she'd recount later to her colleagues.

The woman, tiring of Norman, pointed him toward a dim hallway.

He weaved through the tables, avoiding the curious stares. Across the room, the woman at the door whispered to a coworker, a short woman in a red strapless dress carrying an empty drink tray. Both stared at Norman and laughed.

Turning his back to them, Norman lifted the phone and dialed Cameron's number. On the fourth ring, Erica answered.

"Erica, I need to speak with Cameron."

"Who is this?"

Suddenly Norman heard an eruption of sound behind him, a twangy country song with a sharp steel guitar, clapping, voices shouting over the steady beat of drums. Norman cupped his hand against the phone. "This is Norman." He paused. "Norman Reeves."

"Cameron isn't here," she said. "Call back later."

Her voice began to fade, so Norman had to shout. "Wait, don't hang up. Erica, please." Then he told her about the trip, about the car and the mechanic, and how he needed a ride. "Come and get me," he said. "As soon as possible."

"What gives you the right to order me around?" Erica said. "After all we've done for you. And not even the courtesy of a thank you."

Norman was stunned. "I don't understand," he said.

"When you stayed with us," Erica said, "you never once did the dishes, never vacuumed the floor, never cleaned the bathroom, or paid a bill. All you did was sit around and talk about how horrible the world is. Did you know your mom used to call Cameron every month practically in tears, begging him to help you, to set you up with a nice girl? Too good for everyone, aren't you, Norman? Find your own way home."

At that moment a hand clamped onto Norman's shoulder and spun him around. Immediately Norman recognized the face, the dark eyes and the yellow teeth.

"Of all the places," Curly said, his words thick and slurred, his breath sour. "I never thought I'd find a good boy like you here." He draped his arm over Norman's shoulder.

"I need to go," Norman said. He tried to lift Curly's arm, but it held him tightly.

Curly waved to a woman across the room. "Marta, bring a Coke for my boy Norm. No, too strong? Bring a Sprite."

Three women, all wearing short red dresses that glittered in a false and irritating way, circled the tables with trays of drinks. Another woman sat on a man's lap, head thrown back, laughing, her hand kneading his arm. The black curtain was open. Norman saw a long hallway. A door was open. There was a bed and a black light.

"Please," Norman said. He suddenly felt sick. "I need to go."

Curly put two fingers in his mouth and whistled. "Everyone, this is my friend, Norm, one of those Utah boys, voted nicest in his high school class. His car broke down, so he's a little stuck at the moment, but while here he's chosen the finest entertainment in town."

The room erupted in a chorus of shouts and wolf calls. A few men lifted their glasses.

"Your friend needs to loosen up," one waitress shouted over the music. Norman could see dark freckles on her chest. They reminded him of constellations. "Maybe I can put a smile on his face."

Again the room erupted in cheers. Norman stared at the smiling faces and felt as if his mind had shrunk into something no larger than a pebble.

Lifting a sweaty glass of beer to his lips, Curly said, "Well, what do you say? Ain't that hospitality?"

"I don't feel well," Norman said. He turned for the door. Curly's arm slackened on his shoulder.

"What do you mean?" Curly said. "Why'd you come here in the first place?" He set his glass down and took a step toward Norman. "You don't have no explaining to do, Norm. You're with friends. No one's going to tell, and no one's going to care."

Norman didn't turn back when he heard a crescendo of laughter and boos. He opened the door and decided that he was doing the right thing.

Norman walked toward the motel, passing a bar with a wagon wheel suspended over the door. Through the window, he watched a dozen couples, hands clasped together, faces touching, waltzing across the wooden floor. He needed to call someone but knew that no one would give him a ride. They'd make excuses. They wouldn't answer. They'd delete his message. Norman touched the bar's brass doorknob and paused. The plaintive notes of a piano drifted through the door, a sad melody that yanked at something in the back of his throat.

Norman began to cry, and so as not to be heard or seen, he covered his face with his hand and turned from the window. His body shook as if with convulsions. He'd never felt so alone. And then, with a stone-cold clarity that razored into him, Norman knew he couldn't remember not feeling alone. There had been Carolyn, the girls he dated in high school and college, mission companions and roommates, the people he worked with, friends from home like Cameron. Hadn't they been friends, conversed together, shared memories? A chill inched up Norman's spine, passed through his trembling shoulders, and settled into his jaw, making his teeth chatter. They were his friends, Norman knew, yet he'd always felt comforted he'd avoided their pitfalls and vices, and evaded their unhappiness. Norman wiped at his eyes. Then why am I so unhappy? he thought.

At that moment, Norman saw Maggie walking up the street. A short, overweight man with thinning hair and lardy skin followed her.

"What do you mean you're waiting for your boyfriend?" the man said. "Just one drink. It's not going to hurt no one. You're the cutest little thing I ever seen in this town."

Norman was about to turn away when Maggie waved.

"Play along," she whispered when he was close enough to hear. She held Norman's hand and turned to the man. "Get lost," she said. Norman stood a little taller and glared at the man, who shrugged and walked the other direction. Norman looked down at their hands, at Maggie's fingers intertwined with his. Her hand was soft and warm, and he didn't want to let it go. Maggie smiled and brushed a strand of hair out of her face. He gently squeezed. She squeezed back. What am I doing? Norman thought. He slowly released her hand and stepped back.

"Thanks," Maggie said. "We get some real creeps passing through."

"My pleasure," Norman said. He could smell Maggie's perfume. It came to him in small bursts. He wanted to close his eyes and breathe it in.

"Hey, tough luck with the car," she said. "Lou told me what happened."

"Some things you don't see coming," Norman said. "What a place to be stranded." He realized what he'd said sounded harsh. "I don't mean to criticize your town. It just hasn't been a good day."

"No need to apologize," Maggie said. "Sometimes I feel this place is the end of the world, but it does have its redeeming qualities. And hey, at least we met. Call it serendipity. Well, maybe not." She puffed her cheeks and then raised her arms, letting them fall to her sides. "Okay, I'll confess. Lou told me what direction you went, and I started looking. Do you think that's strange? I usually don't do this. Gee, to be stuck in a strange town, not knowing anyone. I felt bad." She tapped her bottom teeth with her thumb nail and gazed up at Norman. Her blue eyes seemed to take him in at a glance, his utter melancholy and loneliness, his helplessness. "Hey, why don't you come over for dinner? I just live around the corner. It won't be anything special. Come on. What do you say?"

The street lamps buzzed overhead. Norman looked down Main Street toward the blinking casino lights. Beyond the lights he saw nothing but darkness. The thought of walking in that direction seemed unbearable. So did the thought of lying in a motel room, surfing channels, and listening to the rush of cars and trucks on the interstate.

"I am hungry," Norman said.

Maggie's house was small, a bathroom, bedroom, kitchen, and living room sparsely furnished with a blue denim couch and a square slate-top coffee table. Next to the door hung a collage of photographs in a black wooden frame. Several potted plants, arranged according to size, sat on the windowsill. "This is it," Maggie said. "Stand in the middle of the living room, spin once, and you've seen everything. Just give me a second." She disappeared into the kitchen.

The refrigerator opened and closed. The oven door banged shut. There was the click of a turning dial and then the hiss of gas. Norman waited by the front door, touching the ring case in his pocket.

"You can set your backpack down," Maggie said, reappearing so suddenly that her voice startled him. "Make yourself at home."

Norman set the backpack near the door, loosening and then tightening the shoulder straps for no reason at all. The evaporative cooler turned on and rattled through a vent above the bedroom door. On the other side of the room, Maggie stood near the window. She twisted a yellowed leaf from one of the potted plants and rubbed it between her fingers. "I believe in being honest," she said.

Norman waited for some kind of revelation, that Maggie was married or had brought him here to sell him something. "So do I," Norman said.

But Maggie said nothing. Instead, she lifted her pant leg, yanked at a strap cinched around her lower thigh, and removed the leg below the knee. She took the leg, with the shoe still attached, and set it under the coffee table. Then she looked at Norman. "Do you mind?"

"I don't mind," Norman said, watching how the empty pant leg swayed slightly in the blast of air from the vent, surprised, really, that he didn't mind.

"I don't want to make you uncomfortable," Maggie said. "That's why I asked. People can be cruel. You wouldn't believe what they'll say and do. Total strangers, too. Some guy in Elko, right in the middle of Walmart, wanted me to show him how the prosthetic went on. One guy said he'd pay me fifty dollars if he could rub the end of my leg. I don't wear shorts anymore. Even in the middle of summer. You can understand why, I'm sure."

There was something beautiful in her vulnerability, in the way she stared at the floor, shaking her head and smiling bemusedly at people's thoughtlessness and cruelty. Suddenly, Norman wanted to hold Maggie and comfort her. The unexpectedness of this desire shocked him. Norman wondered if he should leave. He ran his hands over his eyes, as if that might help him decide, and then he stared out the window. The thought of walking in that darkness terrified him.

"When I'm home I like to be myself," Maggie said. She hopped to the couch with one graceful leap and sat down. "If you're a floor person, I have pillows. I had the carpets shampooed a few weeks ago."

"I'll just sit by you," Norman said. As an afterthought, he took his shoes off and set them near the prosthetic. "That's better," he said, and then leaned back.

"I knew you wouldn't mind," Maggie said.

"Really, I don't," Norman said, feeling undeserving of Maggie's admiration. "I'm glad you're comfortable."

"I'll admit it's not always easy," she said. "Sometimes, even after ten years, I still cry about it. In high school a friend and I were driving back home from Elko when a drunk driver hit us. That's how it happened: out of nowhere, two headlights and then silence. My friend walked away. I didn't." Maggie rested her arm on the back of the couch. "My parents didn't have health insurance. The whole town helped. Maybe that's why I stay. On the outside people here seem rough and uneducated, but on the inside they're good."

"It must have been quite the community effort," Norman said.

"It was," Maggie said. "For a while I wasn't doing well. Just imagine, one day I'm running track, and the next I can't even stand up. And on top of that, all the hospital bills and the physical therapy. That's when everyone chipped in. After that I always swore I'd help someone if I had the chance. That's why I came back."

With an agility that impressed Norman, Maggie lifted herself from the couch and took the collage of photographs off the wall. She set it on the coffee table and pointed to a picture of a bearded, heavyset man with a rifle slung over his shoulder. Behind him the flat, monochrome desert stretched to the mountains. Norman looked at the other pictures: Maggie playing the piano in a white dress, baking a cake, running track. Norman wondered why the bearded man occupied the center of the collage.

"Your father?" Norman asked.

"No. A friend of the family," Maggie said. "Bill Mortensen." She brushed away a speck of dust on the glass. "He was the third guy at the garage, until he got sick. Cancer. Three packs a day, unfiltered. I saw the X-rays of his lungs. The cancer was like wisps of smoke in there, like smudges. I was living in Colorado at the time, working, taking classes when I wanted, drifting, and then one day my mom called to tell me that Bill was getting worse. She'd been trying to take care of him but could only do so much." Maggie paused. Her lower lip trembled. "It was one of those moments. It sounds so silly, I know. A moment of clarity, as if the universe opened itself for a second and I saw a pathway, a purpose. So I followed it and came home." Maggie wiped at her eyes and smiled. "Gosh, I don't know why I'm telling you this. You must think I'm so gloomy."

"I don't think that at all," Norman said. "You did something most people wouldn't do."

"Maybe," Maggie said, "but I didn't know what I was getting into. It was the typical story of someone dying of cancer. He lived a year beyond the diagnosis. We got into the chemotherapy routine. They called it 'daycare' at the clinic. There was always a wait. Then the drip in the arm. Then the inevitable nausea. It was the most helpless I'd ever felt, watching him puke his guts out and crying, a big, powerful man. Then the cancer got to his liver and then to his brain. There's this horror watching someone you've known all your life deteriorate. Our conversations became shorter. He forgot things. The last forty-eight hours were the worst. My parents were there. Bill's brother, too. By that time we had a nurse. I remember his breathing, like a squeaky door opening and shutting every time he took a breath. It's like it went on forever. At one point the nurse wanted us to leave so she could clean him up. That's when he passed, when we were standing outside the room. It's like he knew we were out of the room and wanted to save us from the final moment."

"Awful," Norman muttered, wincing at how trivial and common the word sounded. He could imagine the shaded room, the raw smell of sickness, the shrunken, waxy figure on the bed, and Maggie standing there, weeping quietly. Norman remembered a phrase he'd read and underlined in a college textbook seven years ago. "There is a great sadness pushing at the world," it said, "and it only needs a little slipway, a little opening." The words seemed rife with meaning, and Norman, for the first time, thought he understood the implication of those words.

"Have you ever read *The Prophet* by Khalil Gibran?" Maggie asked. "I mention it because you're a guidance counselor and help people."

Norman knew the book, the story of an old sage imparting pearls of wisdom, but he'd never read more than a page or two, though many people had recommended it. The story seemed too contrived, too feel-good and saccharine, one of those books that litters thrift stores after its initial popularity has waned. "I haven't," Norman said.

Maggie stood and took a worn blue copy of *The Prophet* from the book shelf next to the door. There was a gold hand stamped on the cover, and in the palm of the hand stood human silhouettes stretching their arms upward. "My English teacher gave me this after the accident," Maggie said. "After reading it, I started writing my own poetry. And then when Bill got sick I bought him a copy. Every day we read a chapter and talked about it. I want to read you something. This was Bill's favorite." She cleared her throat and began. The poem was about pain, how pain breaks a shell that encloses our understanding, how pain, like joy, is one of the miracles of our lives, how we must accept pain just as we accept the seasons of the year because pain's the bitter potion the physician uses to heal us. Maggie barely glanced at the page.

Norman tried to smile as she read, knowing that nothing he had ever thought or said had been as powerful. In all his time as a guidance counselor, he'd never helped anyone the way Maggie had helped Bill.

"You're beautiful," Norman said. "I mean more than just the way you look."

Maggie touched the gold hand on the book's cover. "Thanks," she said.

"You write poetry?" Norman asked. He suddenly wanted to hear her reading something.

"I dabble in it," Maggie said, "but it's awful stuff. I'm embarrassed."

Norman touched her hand. "Read something."

"Okay," Maggie said. She took a worn spiral notebook from under the coffee table. "I read this at Bill's funeral. It's called 'Joy and Sorrow.' You might think it's too depressing. Maybe I'll read something else."

"I'd like to hear it," Norman said.

Taking Norman's hand, Maggie said, "I love the way you look at me." And then she began to read.

Norman closed his eyes and listened. The words were simple and the rhythm somewhat forced, but he enjoyed the poem and even began to believe what Maggie was saying: that the deeper we are cut by sorrow, the deeper our joy, and that joy and sorrow are inseparable, and without them life is empty.

When Maggie finished, she closed the notebook. "You keep doing that," she said, pointing to Norman's hand clamped tightly over his pant pocket.

Norman pulled the ring case from the pocket and examined its polished surface.

"California," Maggie said. She let go of Norman's hand and touched the notebook's metal spiral.

"I don't know if I want to go to California," Norman said. He set the ring case on the coffee table.

"What do you want?" Maggie asked.

"What do I want?" Norman said, more to himself than to Maggie. He reached for her hand. "I want you to read another poem," he said. "I want you to read all of them."

Maggie stared at their clasped hands and nodded. She opened the notebook to the first page and read.

Outside, the wind had picked up, and somewhere in the distance Norman heard chimes ringing, a dreamy melody that seemed to emanate from the earth itself. Sitting beside Maggie, who seemed so beautiful, Norman understood that everything, if examined closely enough, is beautiful. Norman closed his eyes. My life's going to change, he thought.

Enclosure

Lost in Furniture Land

For B.

S. follows blue signs through wide, luminous aisles. *Shortcut to Home Organization. To Bookcases, Media & Storage.* Each, it seems, leads him deeper into this sprawling furniture labyrinth.

He wonders how long ago he pulled into that immense parking lot with vague intentions of buying a few things for his apartment: a side table, a reading lamp, a shower mat. Four hours, eight hours, twelve? An unpleasant realization solidifies in S.'s fatigued mind: he's lost in Furniture Land.

"Excuse me," S. calls out to a Furniture Land employee, a tall, blonde girl in khakis and a blue collared shirt. "The exit," he asks. "Which way. . ."

The girl opens a large glass case and then pushes a red button that stops a metal piston from hissing down on a padded wooden chair. *Resilient!*, a sign above the chair reads. *100% cotton cover. Clear lacquered birch veneer. Only $99.00!* "Hey, you mind giving me a hand?" the girl asks S. "With all this poking, these demo chairs don't last more than a day. My manager Gustav's always telling me to get the goddamn chair the hell out of here by ten or everyone will see it's junk."

She smiles, and for a moment S. forgets the searing pain on the tip of his big toe, the annoying stitch in his upper back, and his overwhelming need to escape Furniture Land. Appraising her Nordic beauty—the sharp nose and soft jawline, platinum hair, and skin like honey—S. is happy to oblige.

Together they carry the chair.

"Hedda," he says, reading her nametag. "That's an unusual name. Swedish?"

"It's not my real name," she says. "All new hires are assigned a Swedish name."

"What's your real name?" S. asks, stepping over a powder-blue footstool. His pant leg catches on one of the stool's sharp corners and tears.

Hedda doesn't notice. She stops and stares up at the recessed lighting. "My real name? I have a childhood memory of my mother calling me Elizabeth. Or was it Katherine? I don't remember. I work a lot. Gustav says I'm on track to win Employee of the Year. He says he'll personally write the recommendation and then sing my praises to the head honchos in the front office. Winners fly to Stockholm to meet The Founder, Viggo Kamprad. I'll have to buy a new dress. I've heard he likes medieval peasant garb."

S. watches moisture pool in Hedda's magnificent blue eyes. A single tear trickles down her cheek and splashes onto her collar. "I want to tell him how much his *Furniture Manifesto* changed my life," she says.

Hedda opens a metal hatch on the wall. The word *Incinerator* is stenciled on its smooth blue surface. S. feels heat on his cheeks, smells burning garbage. The chair slides down a dark tube toward a distant orange glow.

S. wants to ask where the tube goes, but the walkie-talkie on Hedda's hip crackles to life.

"Hedda," the voice screams through a burst of static. "Hedda. . . breakroom in two shakes. . . my back in knots. . . bring me a Coke."

"Gustav," Hedda says as she closes the incinerator hatch. She draws back a curtain on the wall and pushes open a door that says *Employees Only.* "Thanks for the help," she says.

S. steps forward, raises his hand. "Hey, I'm S." He clears his throat, straightens his spine. "I— Maybe tomorrow we could go for a coffee? I just moved here."

The smile vanishes from Hedda's face. Her mouth hangs open. S. wonders if he's offended her. Has she misunderstood his intentions?

"S.," she says, her face pained and contorted, "you mean abandon my post? What would Gustav say? Who would bring his Cokes? He'd be thirsty and irritable. It'd be the end of Employee of the Year. Hilmar over in Rugs will win. I'd never meet Viggo Kamprad." Hedda stops and stares at S. Her face softens. She takes his hand. S. feels a thrill in her warm touch that ripples through his groin. "Oh," she says, "you're attracted to me. You think I'm beautiful. You're asking me out. That's sweet." She runs her hand across S.'s cheek. "I want you to know," she says, "that you're my favorite customer. I mean that."

And then the walkie-talkie buzzes again. "Hedda," the voice screams. "My back. Killing me. Coke. So thirsty."

Hedda turns to go into the employee door.

"Wait," S. says. "What's your number?"

"Call me here," she says. "Tell the operator to transfer you to Couches and Chairs."

"I will," S. says. "I'll call tomorrow." He looks around, smiling dumbly. "Hey, how do I get out of here?"

"You're silly," Hedda says.

"No," S. says. "Really. Where's the exit?"

"Easy," Hedda says. "Go over to Cooking and Eating. Take the shortcut to Lighting. Don't go right or you'll end up in the warehouse. Youth Rooms, Kitchen, shortcut to Decoration and then the left staircase down to Bathrooms. Goodnight, S."

A little bounce in his step, S. plods on toward Cooking and Eating. He can't stop thinking about Hedda. What a smile! What professional commitment and work ethic! And didn't she call him her favorite? Maybe she can plug him into the social scene, get him out of his drab apartment and into one of those Scottsdale nightclubs he's seen on late-night TV. The thought cheers S. But where's that short-cut to Lighting? Why is he in Shoe Racks and Drawer Organization? Has he missed a turn?

S. walks on. More appliances and couch displays. More blue signs. S. looks down at the tear in his pant leg. It's wide enough to put his hand through, wide enough to see the blotchy white psoriasis on his knobby kneecap. And where the hell is everyone? The lights are still on, the canned music still looping through the speakers. But no customers.

And suddenly, not looking where he's going, S. practically falls over the extended footrest of an overstuffed maroon recliner. A black man sits in it, broad shoulders, thighs like tree trunks.

"*Hälningar, kamrat*," the man says, regarding S. through a pair of pink plastic reading glasses. He wears tapered jeans and a faded gray sweatshirt, both too small for his large frame. A striped red and white scarf is knotted around his neck. A thick book is open on his lap. "*Vackra natten en promenade*?"

"I don't understand," S. says.

"Oh." The man looks S. up and down. "You must be new," he says in English, extending his hand. "Kwame Jackson. What's your name?"

S. tells him.

"You look exactly like a guy who lives in Home Organization," Kwame says. "Don Cooley. Nice enough, but he cheats at cards."

"You work here?" S. asks.

Kwame throws his head back and laughs, a deep baritone his enormous chest amplifies. "Work here?" He runs a finger under his dripping eyes. "I bet you think I'm the big black bad-ass who moves the furniture at night. Right? Lazing around while the Boss Man out. Me's sorry, Master Sir. Me's was taking a break. Hell nah. I don't work here. I live here, son."

"You live here?" S. says, hearing panic in his voice. This man is insane, a lunatic, perhaps even dangerous, S. assumes. Someone needs to call security to cart him off in a straightjacket and return him to the nuthouse. S. steps back. "I'm looking for the exit."

"Can't help you there, brother," Kwame says. "Couldn't help, even if I wanted to help. I'm horrible with directions, and I bet you are, too." He closes the book on his lap, removes his reading glasses and taps them on his chin. "Oh, I get it, man, your first day. Cooley whimpered for a week when he got here, kept saying he had bills to pay, that there was no one to feed his Weimaraners. He got over it. Says he's never been happier."

"This is ludicrous," S. says. His head aches, his eyes burn. "What about your job? Don't you have a family?"

Kwame makes a sweeping motion with his hand. "Good riddance." He lifts the book from his lap and delicately balances it on his palm. "Vilhelm Moberg's *History of Sweden.* I just started the second volume. Wars and wars and suffering peasants. Kings and bigwigs treading on the masses. Henpecked husbands. I'm checking out of that history. I'm done with it."

Kwame opens his book and eases back in the chair. "I've chosen a simple life, reading sixteen hours a day. Politics, sports, cooking, history, all Swedish of course, but they're a fascinating people. And what else? Bathrooms everywhere. If I need to shower, I duck into the employee locker room. When my clothes wear out, I hit the Lost and Found." Kwame wags a finger at S.'s torn pants. "You in the market for some new threads, my man? Just yesterday I saw some nice Eddie Bauer slacks in the Lost and Found."

S. doesn't answer. He scans the panels of fluorescent lights above his head, follows the dizzying network of metal tubes hanging from the concrete ceiling. S. fully expects the host of *So We Got You* to emerge from a secret door, bad suit and bad hair, grinning ear to ear as he points to the hidden cameras.

Kwame squints down at his watch. "Dinnertime," he says. "Every night at eleven the cook tosses out the leftovers. I recommend the meatballs with lingonberry sauce. The vegetarian lasagna's not bad. But I wouldn't touch the lox. Fishy as hell."

S. runs his fingers through his hair. "This is crazy. You're crazy. I'm not living here. I start a new job tomorrow. I have obligations." He thinks of the aquarium he bought only yesterday, or was it the day before, of the glass catfish and blue gourami sliding through the bubbling water. Who will feed them? They'll devour each other if he doesn't get home.

S. turns. "I'm getting out of here," he calls over his shoulder.

S.'s brown loafers slap against the laminate flooring. Sweat pours down his neck. A dark spot widens around his crotch and inches toward his waistline. S. runs all night, into the morning and afternoon, into the evening. What day is it? He doesn't know.

Customers regard S. curiously and move to let him pass.

Breathless, S. finally stops in front of a long row of tall windows dark with night and stares at himself, hardly recognizing the slovenly figure with the crazed expression gawking back at him. He inches closer to the thick glass and peers down at the spattering of cars in the parking lot. Beyond it, a line of red taillights traces the serpentine highway that twists and turns through the moonlit desert toward the city's umber haze. S. cups his hand against the glass and squints into the farthest corners of the parking lot, and there it is, his forlorn red Cavalier attached to the backend of a tow truck. The tow man, in shades and mechanic's coveralls, talks on a phone, then bends over double and slaps his knee as he works the hydraulics that lift the small car's front end.

"No!" S. shouts, pounding his palms against the glass. He looks around, lifts a metal swivel chair above his head and hurls it at the window. It bounces off the glass and shatters into pieces around his feet. And then the tow truck is gone, a pair of taillights speeding toward the city.

"Be calm," S. tells himself. His hands tremble. His mind grasps for solutions. What had he learned in Cub Scouts? Don't panic when lost. Direct yourself by locating the moss on a tree, which always grows on the north side. Follow a stream to a river, the river to the ocean. Look to the heavens. Follow the North Star. S. sees no stars, no moss, no stream. But there is a stream of customers, a trickle at this late hour, meandering through the wide aisles toward checkout and the exit beyond. S. has a plan.

Across the aisle, a young couple enters the Dining Room Wing. S. tails them closely, turning away and feigning interest in the grain of table tops or the structural integrity of chairs if they happen to look his way. The fierce fluorescent lighting reflects in the man's oily black hair and off his pointed leather loafers. The woman, her golden hair in a ponytail, wears a pair of black stretch-pants and high brown leather boots. She looks as if she's just competed in some equestrian event.

The woman glances at S. and her smile vanishes. She whispers something to the man, who looks back before taking the woman by the elbow and leading her toward the next row of tables. S. follows.

Quickly, the man turns. "Hey, buddy," he says, pressing his knuckle into S.'s sternum, "we already told your friend outside we wouldn't sign his petition. To tell you the truth, we're a little tired of you tree huggers. I couldn't care less about your sacred red squirrel and spotted owl. I'd eat them for breakfast if somebody served them up. Wouldn't I, honey?"

"He would," the woman says, peeking around the man. "In Liberia, he once ate an entire pygmy hippo, shot it and ate it right down to the bones."

"That's right," the man says. "I'm the hunter. None of this passive-aggressive shit, like annoying people for signatures or tossing cream pies at CEOs. What's that gotten you? If I were you, I'd be jabbing my thumb into some senator's eyeball or breaking his kid's kneecaps with an axe handle. The only thing in this world that gives orders is balls. You understand what I'm saying? You ever seen *Scarface*? That's what I live by."

S. raises his hands in the air. "I'm just trying to get out. That's all I want."

"Do you hear that, honey?" the man says to the woman. "He wants out." He rests his hand on S.'s shoulder. "So you've reached the end, seen the light at the end of the tunnel? You're tired of the ashrams and the communes, lentil soups and chicks with hairy legs. I bet you want to tear into a big Porterhouse without someone calling you a monster. You want to be rich. You want power. You want to be like me. But look at you! Those pants, that shirt! You smell like a taco. You remind me of this homeless guy my fraternity brothers and I enjoyed beating with baseball bats. Call me when you're through with your hippie life. I'll put you in my downline selling spray-on contraceptives. The Latinos are buying them up like hotcakes right now. But until then"—the man waves a fist in S.'s face—"until then, stop cramping us with your hippie stench and hand-me-down clothes, or I'll call security."

A cog turns in S.'s dulled brain. A tumbler locks into place.

"Security," he says. "Yes, call security. Tell them to take me away. Tell them I'm mentally ill. Tell them I'm a pervert."

S. considers spending an hour in Furniture Land jail, concocting some lame excuse about forgetting to take his medication, and then being escorted out into that beautiful heat and desert air.

"Always looking for a platform, aren't you?" the man says. He turns to the woman. "I wouldn't give him the satisfaction, would I, honey?"

"He wouldn't," the woman says. "He never gives satisfaction."

"No," the man says. He jerks his head to the side. His neck vertebrae crackle. "But right now there's one thing that would give me some satisfaction."

"Baby, you're so bad," the woman says. She licks her lips. "Such a bad baby."

And now the man and woman are on S., their fists hammering at his face and stomach. S. is down on the laminate floor, hands shielding his face, knees pulled up to his chest. The woman shrieks and repeatedly drives the heel of her brown riding boot into the soft flesh covering S.'s tailbone. The man, breathing heavily, rams a clear plastic cylinder meant to hold pasta into the back of S.'s head. "So you want to dance?" the man says. "Say goodnight to the bad guy! Say goodnight!"

S. screams. His limbs jerk and jump. There's an undulating blackness around the edges of things, then darkness and silence.

S. awakens in bed, every muscle and joint aching. A beautiful incandescent light surrounds him. What a nightmare, he thinks, burrowing deeper into a goose-down comforter. Somewhere above him, he hears the scratch of a pen on paper. His eyes snap open. A man in a white lab coat, stethoscope tucked into his breast pocket, stands at the foot of the bed, scribbling on a clipboard. S. feverishly absorbs his new surroundings. White floors, white ceilings, white fluorescent lights, beds with white sheets as far as the eyes can see, row after row of them, all occupied by sleeping, supine bodies.

"I'm Doctor Kröken," the man says, clicking the top of his pen before sliding it into his breast pocket. "We had a betting pool on when you'd wake up," he says. "It seems Doctors Framtid and Luftig owe me a Coke." He searches the clipboard. "A Mr. Jackson brought you in. You're lucky he found you, Mr.—" Kröken covers his mouth and snorts a dry laugh. "We've been calling you Mr. Scruffy-Pants. It's just a little game we sometimes play. No harm. But anyway, someone assaulted you, stuffed you under a futon, left you for dead. Nasty business. Unfortunately, there's been a bit of a criminal element in Dining, a lot of shopping-related stress. We're cracking down on it."

S. raises up on his elbow. "What do you mean? Where am I? Is this Good Samaritan? Saint Joseph's?"

Kröken smiles. "Heavens no. Those hospitals are so third world. Filthy. Medieval. You're a patient in the Furniture Land Clinic. Last year the Swedish Medical Association awarded us the Golden Herring Award for our optimal care."

S.'s mouth opens.

"Oh, don't worry about the cost," Kröken says. "It's all taken care of. You're very important to us. We need color in your cheeks, a pleasant grin on your face. We need you out on that sales floor projecting an air of satisfaction and comfort."

"What the hell are you talking about?" S. says. He gazes at the acres of sleeping bodies tucked between white sheets, hears the barely audible susurrus of inhaling and exhaling. "I'm not staying here," he says. "You're crazy."

Kröken appears offended. "Don't want to stay?" he says. "Do you feel that goose-down comforter, that Hagavik active-response coil mattress? Think of your life here: not a care in the world. A life of ease and comfort. Have you experienced the massage recliners? Have you tried the Swedish meatballs? The coffee?"

"I'll be on my way," S. says, kicking off the comforter. He stands, swaying slightly. And what is he wearing? Some kind of hospital gown. "If you'll be kind enough to show me to the exit," S. says, suddenly winded. "No. Don't a say a word. I'll find it myself." The hospital gown gapes in back. A cold draft slides across S.'s left buttock.

"Wait," Kröken says. "You're in no condition to walk. Look at your vitals"—he waves the clipboard in S.'s face—"and your mangled face. You'll scare customers."

"Thank you," S. says, "but no thank you. Goodbye." He totters on the balls of his naked feet, takes an uncertain step forward, blinks quickly. Brilliant bursts of white light dance in the air.

"You leave me no choice," Kröken says. He snaps his fingers and two hulking men in white uniforms appear from behind a curtain, thick jaws with barely a trace of blond stubble on their dimpled chins, deep-set expressionless eyes.

"Back off," S. says. He shuffles toward a set of double doors.

Kröken holds a syringe in his left hand. "Why don't you lie down? We'll talk about this."

S. looks back as he runs for the doors. "Get away from me." S. reaches the doors, pushes the handle. No give. Nothing. S. turns. The goons approach.

"Locked," Kröken says. "Now how about something to help you sleep?"

S. looks up to the ceiling, then down at the floor. He leans against the wall. His hand grazes something smooth and metallic. A handle? A square blue hatch marked *Incinerator*?

"Not wise," Kröken says. He pinches the syringe between his fingers, turning it in small circles. "A conflagration. You'll be incinerated. Your ashes will fall from the sky."

S. pulls the hatch open and stares down into the black tube. No trace of heat, no faint fiery glow. And before S. can process his actions, he's sliding down the tube, faster and faster through the darkness. His screams reverberate around him. And then he's on the ground, somersaulting through pillowy mounds of gray ash. It coats his skin. Great tears roll down his cheeks. And what is this place? A room? A furnace? Four cinder block walls, an iron door with a square glass window, piles of ash, and the metallic skeletons of recliners, couches, and love seats. Coughing, S. limps toward the door, looking back once at the great metal tube, expecting the goons to slide out.

The heavy door creeks open. S. moves down a narrow cement hallway toward a faint emerald glow. His tailbone's sore. His left eye throbs. After a few minutes of walking, he stops and rubs his eyes. What does he see? A mirage? A hallucination? Can it be real, this illuminated exit sign above a metal door? S. is giddy. He's never felt such joy. He runs for the door, pushes it open and enters the night. The air, heavy with desert scents, is like a furnace. The concrete burns under his feet. But S. doesn't care. He's free.

The black macadam of the empty parking lot stretches out before him. S. blinks, regards his crumpled hospital gown streaked with ash, dances on his heels. Out there beyond the empty parking lot is the city's dim glow. His apartment is there, his fish. Thirty miles of asphalt to home. It will take an iron will to walk that distance, but S. is up for the challenge. He steps off the curb. Suddenly the door behind him opens.

Hedda stands there, as fresh as the first time S. saw her, not a stain on her khakis, not a blonde hair out of place. She tips her head up to admire the enormous Furniture Land sign fixed to the building. Her face is bathed in a pale yellow light. "I've always loved that color," she says, fingering the walkie-talkie on her hip. "It reminds me of summer. It comforts me."

S. doesn't look up. "You said I was your favorite."

The walkie-talkie crackles and then a voice squawks, "Hedda. Ibuprofen. Spasm. Coke." Hedda looks down at the walk-talkie for a moment, then turns a knob that kills the voice. "S.," she says, moving forward to touch his arm, "sweet S. You are my favorite. You'll always be my favorite." She looks over his shoulder at the winding road beyond the parking lot. The full moon reflects in her eyes. "You sure you want to travel that long road?" she asks. "And what's at the end? Do you ever think about that? Those used to be the dark thoughts that kept me up at night."

"What's at the end?" S. stares at the distant city. "What's at the end is life. The real world. This"—S. points to the enormous buzzing sign above—"this isn't real."

Hedda considers this. She nods. "That's right, S." Her voice brims with concession. "You're right. None of this is real. But what about that real world out there, S.? How's that worked out for you?" She smiles and reaches for him. Her open hand reflects the electric yellow light, and S. knows all he has to do is take that hand and follow. "It's easy to forget," Hedda says. "A nice recliner. A good book. Satisfaction and comfort."

"So it's that easy, huh?" S. says.

He scans the horizon. His gloomy apartment is out there, his fish, long expired, he's sure, a new job, maybe. And then S. looks at that hand, Hedda's hand, so soft and beautiful he can never imagine it growing old. Then he feels himself turning, a new kind of turning. No tangle of lines on a map. No bewildering succession of detour signs. Nothing like that. A new feeling.

After All the Fun We Had

Last year kids were just disappearing from our classrooms. Literally. You'd look and there'd be twelve empty seats when there'd only been nine a minute before. They'd sneak out the door, crawl through the windows if they had to. God knows where they went. Sniffing glue in some back alley. Stealing beer from the Gas 'n Go. Those were usually good guesses.

It's not like their parents cared. Our phone calls irritated them. They'd tell us to go you-know-what and hang up.

And the few students who managed to stick around? About an hour of consciousness, until the Red Bull and Adderall wore off, and then they'd pass out and slobber all over the desktops. Teachers complained. "We're white noise," they'd shout at me in staff meetings. "We can't break through all the apathy."

"Calm down," I'd tell them. "Calm down. Some decorum, please."

These crybaby teachers knew as well as I did that we didn't have any leverage with these kids. Still, I threatened to take away the nacho bar and cancel Chicken Nugget Fridays if we didn't see a real change in attitude and a rise in attendance. I drafted an intricate code of conduct and posted one in each classroom: how to sit in a chair, how to properly address a teacher, how to treat a textbook. Students cried oppression and then transferred to other schools. We had too many empty seats. There wasn't enough money coming in from the State. We barely made payroll the last half of the year. We couldn't afford to lose another student.

The problem was that these kids hated school. At best they tolerated it. They couldn't wait to get out on the streets again. I'd hide behind the oleander in the parking lot and catch them crawling under the chain-link fence. I'd lecture them on the value of education and quote statistics about unemployment rates for high school dropouts. They'd stare at me with dreamy, molasses eyes. "We're bored," they'd say. Bored! I was incredulous. It's not like they were headed down to Chase Field to catch the last innings of the Diamondbacks game. They were off to smoke a joint under a freeway overpass or to watch some stupid daytime talk show where people brawl over paternity results.

Something had to change this year—or we wouldn't have a school. What the hell, I told the teachers, if all the oppression and the rules and Chicken Nugget Fridays aren't working, then let's make it fun. Let's sink some money into it. Let's give these kids a reason to come to school. We had our naysayers, I'll admit. We had some teachers who quit outright. But that was all right, because a fun school has to start with the teachers. We had to have some cool teachers.

First, I hired Mr. Dingus. He taught carpentry. A hulk of a man. A jaw like a steel trap. Thighs like stone pillars. He oozed this heady bravado, had a palpable and musky masculinity I thought our students needed. He'd be the father figure, the kindhearted uncle, whatever, an alternative to all the men in these kids' lives who'd never shown up for their birthday parties and basketball games. He wore dark shades in the classroom. He spoke in grunts and clipped phrases. He could lift the backend of a Ford Fiesta. He was the cool teacher. That's what all his students said with a kind of puppy dog look on their faces: "Mr. Dingus is cool."

Then there was Miss Beauchamp. She taught biology. Her wide-ranging resume arrived a week before school started. She had a background in dance and had even done some acting for a small film studio in the San Fernando Valley called Elegant Angel Entertainment. Maybe I'd never heard of her alma mater, some online school in Daytona Beach. Maybe her grades weren't stellar. But we were in a pinch. It was serendipitous. I mean, I knew it during our interview. I kept thinking as I looked at the chiseled contours of her tanned calves and the soft slope of her jaw, kept thinking that such a beautiful specimen was perfect to teach our bored students about homeostasis and cells and photosynthesis and reproduction. She was a breath of fresh air, a stark contrast to Ms. Leverkus, our biology teacher last year, a frail woman who wore ascots and hideous pastel polyester pants. Ms. Leverkus was so old and dried out, so boring and blanched of life, she eerily reminded me of the geriatric corpse I poked and prodded way back when in an undergraduate anatomy lab. No wonder our test scores in the hard sciences plummeted last year. These kids were scared of her. She smelled and looked of death. That gravely smoker's voice, those spotted, veiny hands. She bore a striking resemblance to King Tut's mummified head. Ugh! Anyway, she passed away suddenly in early August from some kind of blood clot or aneurism, which really saved me the inconvenience and awkwardness of firing her.

So we had some cool teachers. Now I had to worry about the first day of school.

I envisioned a party, an event, a beginning-of-the-year celebration these kids would talk about. Not some hot dogs and balloons. Something huge. A festival. A carnival. We had to get the word out, form an identity as a school where education is fun. I hired a place off Camelback Road called Got Party to handle the finer details. I told them to spare no expense.

On the first day of school these kids trickled in, late, as usual, eyes glazed over from a summer of debauchery, stinking of reefer and cheap malt liquor. They stopped at the gates, gaping, taking in the blazing carousel in the back of the parking lot and the full mariachi band trilling near the school's entrance. They were dazed. Some, helplessly enchanted by the carousel's melody, reached into their pockets and pulled out greasy dollar bills, offering them to me. "No need for that," I whispered, leading them through the gates. "Go. Eat. Have fun. This is only the beginning."

We had a hundred students that first day, a hundred and fifty the next, and by the end of the week we'd maxed out our enrollment. I mean, we didn't have an empty seat. We were turning kids away. For the first time we had a waiting list. The money was pouring in: sixty dollars per student per day from the State.

About a month into the first semester I got a phone call from Phillip Begay's mother. He'd come home from school pretty upset. She wanted to know what had happened. I thought Harris Mitchell had been pummeling her little boy again behind the Gas 'n Go. I wished it was that. No, Phillip told her that Miss Beauchamp, at the end of a lecture on the human reproductive anatomy in her all-boys biology class, had drawn a number of lifelike figures on the chalkboard in various sexual positions. I was shocked. Horrified, really. I was speechless. What could I say? I told Ms. Begay we'd look into it immediately, that this was a serious matter, that any harmful contagion would be rooted out—my exact words.

Miss Beauchamp didn't deny it. She cried, she wrung her hands, she wiped at her streaming mascara. I volunteered my handkerchief. God, she was beautiful, like a woman in an old painting who had been taken in sin. Anyway, she was frustrated. Students dozing off, smarting off. She wanted to connect with her students, have a laugh together, be the hip teacher. So when Vincent Lobato shot up his hand at the end of the lecture and asked how to do it, and everyone giggled, she got caught up in the moment. It was a lapse of judgment, a mistake. This was her first teaching job. You know how it is. That first year is tough. Lesson plans, classroom presence, classroom management. And let's face it, most of our students are rude and ungracious. So she drew a few figures on the board, nothing hard-core, really as a joke more than anything else, you know, to get a laugh from the kids. And that was that. There was a rumor that she'd mounted a desk while unbuttoning her blouse and told the class she'd make men of every last one of them before the end of the period. Totally false and ungrounded. Well, we still had to let her go. A real shame. Really.

So we had that little problem with Miss Beauchamp, but our attendance was steady. Students were excited. They wanted to be at school. We had pizza parties, raffles and giveaways, a carnival with clowns and an inflatable castle, a concert on the basketball court by a local rapper who called himself Captain Boolicious.

Well, it got expensive. Yes, we had to adjust our budget. Not everyone was happy, especially our cosmetology teacher, Ms. Hardu. Last year I'd promised her a new classroom with recessed lighting and sinks and fancy chairs for cutting hair, some place she could open to the public so the girls could get their hours. She wanted a Zen-like feel to the room, a bubbling fountain, potted bamboo. It sounded expensive. I tried to reason with her, to show her our full attendance rosters, to speak to the greater good. She wouldn't have any of it. Then it hit me: have Dingus and his advanced carpentry class do it, you know, save a few bucks and let the kids build something bigger than a jewelry box.

"Cool," Dingus said when I told him. He stared at me over his shades. A toothpick hung from his lower lip. "Cool, cool."

Well, they finished in mid-December. Ms. Hardu was ecstatic. She planned this big party, cookies and punch and a cheese platter, and even invited Sterling Couples and Rhonda Felski from the city council to give some prestige to the event, make the kids feel they'd really accomplished something. It was wonderful, all of it, the cheese and the punch and the cookies, right up until the entire interior wall dividing the cosmetology classroom from the salon area came crashing down. You should have seen the chaos, the spilled drinks, plates of cheese and crackers flying through the air, the screaming as students clambered under desks and into doorways. We thought it was an earthquake. Thank God no one was hurt.

Superintendent Flinders was irate, understandably. "Somebody could've been killed," he said. "Somebody could've sued." There was blame to assign, heads to roll. He wanted to know what happened. You know, why the wall fell.

What could I tell him? He knows as well as I do how these kids are. They get excited for about ten minutes when you let them hammer some nails or use the band saw, and then they're bored and want to destroy something.

It turns out some of the boys had gotten hold of the nail gun and started firing it into the roof. I saw the damage myself, hundreds of little holes up there. Looked like an enormous constellation. And of course they had pulled all the nails so they wouldn't get caught. And then we had all that rain. That's how the water got in. It was that second week of December. Three days of rain. Buckets and buckets of it. My laundry room leaked. My wife found black mushrooms growing in our bedroom closet. Anyway, the water got in and saturated the wall.

The rain was understandable, but the real issue was the wall. Superintendent Flinders sent out this inspector to look at the broken mess, and this guy said it was a miracle the wall hadn't gone over sooner. He'd never seen anything like it, two-by-fours, two-by-twos, bailing wire and wood glue, a few nails here and there. In fact, he was surprised the wall had stood at all. Superintendent Flinders wanted to know why Dingus hadn't checked his students' work. He wanted to know if Dingus knew anything about carpentry. Dingus blamed his lazy students and the subpar materials he'd had to use because of the limited budget. We questioned Dingus's T.A., Marvin Sanders, who was tight-lipped about the whole thing and answered our questions with a lot of head-scratching and incoherent mumblings, until we offered him a twenty-five-dollar gift certificate to Applebee's. That really perked him up.

"And why hadn't Dingus checked the students' work?" we asked.

"Well, how could he if he wasn't in the classroom?" Marvin said.

And where had he been, we wanted to know. Marvin said Dingus and Miss Lorraine, the massage therapy teacher, had been doing some repairs in the utility closet behind the stage. Lots of repairs. We found a mattress in there, some personal lubricant and a container of whey protein. Nasty business. Unconscionable. Yes, we fired them. The students took it hard. Dingus was the cool teacher.

These kids circulated a petition to reinstate him, and then a petition calling for my resignation because I'd fired the guy. They didn't get it. They live by a different code. Dingus was having sexual intercourse with Miss Lorraine in the utility closet and in their minds that elevated his status to that of a minor god. For a whole week they grumbled about the injustice of it. But then that Friday we had ice cream and pizza, you know, to smooth over some of that angst. They forgot all about Dingus when they saw the Domino's guy. Thank God these kids have short memories.

Well, we had a few setbacks, but the school year went on, better than expected, I should say. In January we brought in Randy the

Reptile Man, and then there was Spirit Week, then the petting zoo, and then the Valentine's Day dance at the Hyatt Regency. We had the Zapato Family Acrobats in early March. Then Miss Boyle, our world literature teacher, complained that our students weren't getting enough culture and decided to bring in a troupe of Irish dancers. The students quickly booed them off the stage. We made up for it the next week with some street dance team from Los Angeles called Epidemic Crisis. The kids loved them.

And of course every Friday during fifth and sixth period we watched movies and ate pizza. I'd bought a bunch of crap action movies from the discount bin at Walmart: *Quarter to Dead, Killer Piranhas 6, Pirates and Aliens.* But these kids weren't interested in action movies. They just wanted to watch this saccharine Hallmark movie I'd also pulled from the discount bin, thinking my wife would love it, a low-budget piece of drivel about a dysfunctional family who befriends Bigfoot, and that helps them love one another again. These kids couldn't get enough of it. They'd watch it over and over, wiping away tears with grease-stained napkins. That's how these kids are. Just when you think you know them, they surprise you.

Anyway, we were having a great year. Kids were in class, maybe not doing much work, but they were there, they were attentive and courteous, and that counts for something. We finally had leverage. School was fun, a party, and nobody wanted to be left out for some bad behavior. They wanted to be there. They were excited. I could see it in the way they twiddled their cotton candy-stained fingers and smacked their lips. They were always asking me what was next, who was coming to entertain them, when they would eat again. That's why we were so surprised at what happened at the end of April.

It was a Friday afternoon, all the kids gone for the weekend. We were having our staff meeting in the library, hashing out the final details for the school's *Cinco de Mayo* celebration. Ms. Lipton was reporting on the Ferris wheel and big-top tent we'd rented for the occasion, when suddenly we heard a hundred voices out in the hallway. Then these kids started pouring into the library, shouting at us, their faces pinched and angry.

"We've barricaded the school," they said. "No one goes in or out until our demands are met."

I stood there and faced them, and said, not so gently: "What do you have to complain about? We're planning a party for you. Aren't you having fun? Don't you love school now? Last year. Remember last year?"

"We want more than just cotton candy and fire-eaters," they said. "We want you to hug us. We want to be a family."

"There are rules," I said. "There are laws. I can't hold you, I can't touch you. I could be fired. The State could shut us down."

They pressed in on us. A raw, throaty vibration filled the room. I hadn't seen it before, but you know how these kids are: they had baseball bats, knives, and long pieces of chain looped around their hands.

"You'll be the father," they said, pointing to me, and then they pointed to Ms. Lipton, who looked ready to cry. "And you'll be the mother. And you'll both sit in these chairs, and we'll be your children."

So Ms. Lipton and I sat there like stunned fish, staring at the wall.

"No," they told me. "Put your arm around her. Rest your head on her shoulder. Yes, like that." Then Alex Escobar came forward and taped a piece of poster board to the wall: a hand-drawn brick hearth with a blazing fire. And then he put up another poster, a New England winter scene: leafless maples covered with snow, a serpentine lane threading through dark woods to a quaint log cabin with glowing windows.

"We're frightened," they said. "Hold us. Tell us everything will be all right."

They dimmed the lights and sat at our feet. Someone passed around steaming cups of spiced apple cider. They sipped pensively. They sang Christmas carols. I sat there clutching Ms. Lipton's cold hand. Her eyes were pressed shut, her lips moved but no sound came out. If I so much as loosened my grip on her hand, I heard a chain rattle behind me. The hours passed. Above the school I heard the low whir of news helicopters, and from the parking lot the commanding baritone of a police officer shouting into a megaphone.

"This can't go on forever," I told them. I was getting impatient. I had to use the bathroom.

"Shhhhh," they said, their heads resting against our knees. "Just a while longer. We'll be good, we promise. Shhhhhhh."

Suddenly there was an enormous boom and then a blinding flash of light. The ceiling tiles collapsed above the doorway and twenty members of the Phoenix swat team dropped through the hole. The students ran for the door, screaming, vaulting over chairs and tables. The swat team was ready, strafing them with pepper spray and beanbags. The kids crumpled to the floor, squirming there like blinded newborns just pulled from the womb. I watched them with an astonished satisfaction as they rubbed their burning eyes and wept loudly. I took a step forward. I don't know why. I wanted to lecture them, say something about gratitude. But then three members of the swat team lifted me off the ground and whisked me away. My throat burned. I looked back at all those writhing bodies. These kids. So damn ungrateful.

Well, that's what happened, a quarter of our students gone just like that, doing three to six months in Durango. I can't believe it. After all we'd done for them, after all the fun we'd had.

The school will survive. I think. Back to the basics: reading, writing, math. Nothing extracurricular, no pizza parties or carnivals. We'll probably lose another fifty students. Maybe seventy-five. I can already see their bored faces. Who knows, most of them will probably be in Durango within a year anyway.

I've been to these kids' arraignments. I've seen them in court, lost and angry in those silly orange jumpsuits and black canvas slip-ons. I've heard what goes on in Durango—the bland food, those long, bored hours, lights that never turn off. God, I want to shake these kids, ask them if they're having fun in there. But you and I both know I can't touch them.

Our Students

On Friday we readied our classrooms for Monday, the first day of school.

I was arranging desks when one of the returning teachers walked in. Miller. He taught biology across the hall, a tall, freckled man older than my father, in stonewashed jeans and a faded blue T-shirt. "So you and Stephenson are the new meat," he said, extending his hand. "I hope you last longer than the guy you're replacing. His students smelled the fear on his breath. They pounced."

Miller lifted a class roster from my desk and ran his finger down a column of names. "Bad, bad, pregnant, probation, psychopath, bad. Watch this Angel Rodriguez. He's an annoying little shit." He tossed the roster back on the desk. "Hey, some of us are doing lunch. Stephenson already turned me down. You in?"

An hour later we were huddled in a booth at Bill Johnson's Big Apple with two other teachers: Hernandez and Gaines. I'd noticed them, with Miller, sitting together at orientation, exuding a seasoned camaraderie—passing notes, rolling their eyes, and yawning loudly—as Mr. Pitts, the principal, went on about state teaching standards and attendance reports. They'd taught at this place, Pathway to Success Alternative High School, for a few years and had the stories to prove it. They laughed loudly and told their stories with a macabre gallows humor, and I was their audience. Were they trying to impress me or scare me? I didn't know.

"Remember the fat teacher from a couple years back?" Miller asked.

Gaines lifted a sweaty glass to his lips. "Mr. Katz. Yes, enormous. Fat rolls spilling over his belt."

Miller looked at me. "That's right. Katz. Big black guy. Taught business classes. His wife worked in the cafeteria. So one day after school I'm walking past the cafeteria and I hear this woman screaming. I run in there and Katz has his wife in a headlock and he's punching her in the face. Boom, boom. No joke. So I'm wrestling Katz, trying to get his wife out of that headlock, and there's blood dripping from her nose and mouth, and she's screaming, and I'm doing a little dance with Katz, and my shoes are smearing the blood all over the floor. And then Gaines and Hernandez show up, and it's like the three of us are dancing with Katz and his screaming wife, right?"

"His breath," Hernandez said. "Horrible. Like ammonia. That's what shocked me most."

"Yeah, the guy smelled like a gym locker," Gaines said.

"The guy was huge," Miller said, "and you can imagine the three of us swinging from his back like a pack of monkeys. Well, suddenly Katz collapses onto the floor, like somebody flipped a switch on him, and he starts crying like a baby."

"The police carted him off in handcuffs," Gaines said. He clucked his tongue. "Sad."

I chewed my steak but suddenly had no appetite. It sat on my plate in a little pool of blood.

"What do you tell your students?" Miller asked me. "What do you say when they ask what happened to Mr. Katz?"

"You tell them," Hernandez said quickly, grabbing Miller's shoulder, "you tell them to tap twice on the bars if they want their grades."

The three men erupted in titters, and I couldn't help laughing, too. An older woman in the booth next to ours glanced up from her menu and whispered something to her husband. They stood and moved to a table across the restaurant.

I pushed my plate away. Katz. An anomaly, I thought. But Miller went on. Story after story about incompetent teachers and sociopath students: the teacher fired for hiding a student's bag of weed during a drug sweep; the teacher fired for having sex in her classroom with the guy who mopped the floors and took out the trash; the riot in the school's lobby when Hernandez got wonked over the head with a folding chair; the stoned student who'd pissed on the trophy case. These guys reveled in the chaos, accepted whatever absurdity awaited them and the hilarious story it would yield. But from what they told me about themselves, their futures had nothing to do with this run-down charter school. They were biding their time until their real vocations presented themselves. Even old Miller, not far from retirement, was taking a night class in real estate. Gaines had a catering business and painted houses in the summer. Hernandez played bass in a rock band. They were in a holding pattern, weighing their options and planning their escape.

They were the clowns, the comic relief, and because I'd been the clown, in high school, in college, and had always hung out with clowns, I liked them. They wanted to know what I was doing in this shithole. I told them: a year teaching and then law school. They smiled, maybe politely.

"So you want to be a lawyer," Miller said. "Why?"

I chewed on my straw. Why? Because someday I wanted more than the bland middle-class neighborhood I grew up in outside Tucson, the sprawling grid of well-tended lawns and trampolines and minivans. I had fraternity brothers at Arizona State who grew up in Paradise Valley or in those modern homes riding the foothills below Camelback Mountain. Sometimes when their parents were away in Vegas or Acapulco for the week, we swam in their pools and drank Coronas and tequila on stone terraces whose views made me dizzy. Even if you've never wanted for anything, you begin to think differently when you look down on the world like that.

And why was I here, teaching in this dilapidated charter school? Because some of the books I'd read about increasing my chances of acceptance to a top-ranked law program suggested either a stint in the Peace Corps or teaching a year in one of these urban, at-risk charter schools. I didn't have the imagination or the fortitude for three years of third world living, but I liked the idea of teaching. I liked the idea of standing in front of a classroom, lecturing and fielding questions. A year teaching in one of Phoenix's inner-city slum schools—a year seemed doable, if it meant a shot at a more prestigious law school.

But I didn't tell Miller this.

"Why do I want to be a lawyer?" I ran my finger along the edge of the table. "I want to help people."

Hernandez swirled the ice in his empty glass and then waved to our server. Gaines sneezed into his hand and said what sounded like a profanity. Miller just stared at me.

"Come on," Miller said. "Cut the crap. Help people. That's thick. You're insulting us." He smiled. "You want to be rich. Right?"

I shrugged. "Sure. I guess. Don't we all?"

Hernandez slapped me on the back. Miller had his hand on my shoulder. They were all laughing now, and I was laughing, too. But I could see they didn't believe me. They'd heard it before, I was sure, heard it from their own lips maybe. The dreams, the lofty ambitions. But I was serious. A year and no more.

And so the school year began.

The chaos was dizzying. A constant chatter bubbled through the thin walls.

There was the hyperactive, attention-deficient black kid who couldn't stand still, who burst into my classroom in paroxysms of shouts and giggles, mid-lecture, mid-test, like a performer mounting a stage; the morose guy with the full beard who refused to answer my questions, who exuded a latent violence I didn't want to awaken; the three girls in my second period with their stretch-marked breasts practically spilling from their tight V-neck T-shirts, mothers already at fifteen, who couldn't stop smacking their gum and giggling about the boy across the room with the oily hair and gold necklaces. Some of these kids had spent time in jail. Grand theft, drug possession, assault. They had probation officers, wore ankle monitors, got out of school early once a week to go piss in a cup. And I, their teacher, an educator in title only, was responsible for them.

By the end of the first week, I already disliked them. They irritated me with their bored, vacant eyes and incessant chatter about dreams of stardom and wealth. Stardom and wealth! They couldn't even get up in the morning, couldn't even get through a chapter of Arizona history without dozing. They had adult bodies, but the minds of children.

How could I teach them Arizona history? These kids didn't even bring pen and paper. They were absent for days at a time. They showed up high.

I had no training, no certification, no background in pedagogy. But for the first couple of weeks I tried, arriving early in shirt and tie, smiling until my face felt sore from it. I crafted the kind of lessons that interested me at their age: a slide show of Arizona's geologic past, a PBS documentary on Geronimo, articles on current events, group work. My students couldn't care less. Everything was boring. Copying notes was too much. Reading was too much. They quit at the first tinge of discomfort.

Then one day after school, sometime at the end of the second week, I looked up from my lesson plans and Miller was there. He smiled as he ran his fingernails down the length of the chalkboard. "Quittin' time," he said. "We usually go out for a drink. You coming?"

"Lesson plans," I said. "You done already?"

"I'm showing a movie tomorrow. And maybe the next day and the day after." He snapped his fingers. "Let them color some pictures, finger paint, weave baskets. Whatever. Come on. I'll buy the first round."

I looked at my lesson plans, imagined the icy indifference that would greet me the next day, the incessant complaints regardless of how much preparation I put in.

I stood and followed Miller.

We drove to a place called McDuffy's, a dimly lit, decrepit bar off Van Buren with a western motif, an old swinging saloon door and a corrugated metal awning. Gaines was already deep into his fourth beer when we arrived, and Hernandez was on a raised stage near the back wall belting out "Hotel California" into a microphone while the song lyrics scrolled across a large TV screen. A video showed two young lovers with terrified expressions running hand in hand through a maze of dim hallways.

"We aren't teachers," Miller said, when we found a place to sit, and I felt he was talking to me in some veiled, avuncular way, imparting his wisdom. "Teacher's a misnomer. We're babysitters. How are we supposed to discipline these kids?" Miller lifted his beer to his lips without taking his eyes off me. "What leverage do we have? Fifty-five dollars per student per day. That's what the State pays us. Tell Pitts we need to expel some bad seed and you see the dollar signs dance in his eyes. These kids know we can't get rid of them. They know we can't afford it."

Hernandez was still on stage, whipping his head around. The TV screen said *Instrumental: Guitar Solo.* The lovers were locked in a passionate embrace on the hood of a pink convertible Cadillac. Hernandez smiled at us and pumped his fist in the air. We raised our beers and nodded. "He's a horrible singer, isn't he?" Miller said out of the corner of his mouth. "God-awful."

"Such a long song," Gaines said, his hands covering his face. "Terrible. I can't take it." He stood and walked unsteadily to the bathroom.

Miller put his arm around my shoulder and pulled me closer. I felt his warm breath on my cheek. "I know you don't respect me," he said. "You think you're better than me because you'll be out in a year and I'll still be rotting away with these losers. Am I right?"

I tried to say something, but Miller cut me off. "You're right. Guilty as charged. I'm the ship that never left the harbor, the lazy, burned-out teacher. I'll be the first to admit it. Teaching's a gift I don't have. I don't have the desire or the ambition. Years ago when I got into this, there was a guy named Driscoll, old and tired, always at his desk with his face buried in a newspaper. I vowed never to become Driscoll. Teaching was temporary. My calling was elsewhere. I was pre-med in college. I'd been accepted to medical school at Temple. But I knocked this girl up at the end of my senior year. In those days you did the right thing. Today I'd have told her to get an abortion. Then marriage. I deferred a year. And then another kid. Divorce. Child support. Another marriage. No medical school. The years pass quickly, my friend."

Gaines returned from the bathroom. He sat down heavily and looked around, eyes half-closed, his head drooping and then snapping upright. There was a spatter of brown vomit on his shirt cuff.

"Watch this," Miller told me. "Gaines," he said loudly, cupping his hands around his mouth. "Gaines, you're pathetic. Your fattest student wouldn't sleep with you. Your face looks like an ass with a nose and lips." And then Miller slapped him hard across the face. Gaines's head rolled onto his left shoulder. His eyes closed. "He won't remember that," Miller said, lowering Gaines's head slowly onto the oak table.

"Let me tell you something," Miller said. "I mean no disrespect to anyone. I'm no racist. I love all people. You understand? But we're not here to send these kids to college. This is educational triage. Basic skills. Maybe they'll stay out of jail. Maybe a few will manage to pay a rent someday, pay their taxes. That's it. Crossword puzzles. Word finds. Let them paint and color. Show movies. That's what these kids want. It's part of the social contract. They come to these schools because they're easy."

"And Pitts is okay with that?" I asked.

"Crystal clear." Miller jabbed at the table with his index finger. "Busy work. Distraction. Give them A's. Everyone's happy. No complaints. Pitts hates complaints."

I nodded and then looked at Gaines, still passed out on the table.

I felt some relief in what Miller said. As a teacher, I didn't have the desire or ambition he'd spoken about, and I didn't care about acquiring these attributes. I needed to finish the year, and what I heard in Miller's advice was the path of least resistance.

So the next day at lunch I shut myself away, and then the next day and the day after. I ignored the chaos simmering outside my door as I studied for the LSAT. During my prep period and after school I did the same, and then threw together some easy worksheets for class the next day. At four, suddenly thirsty, I'd close my LSAT study guide and wait for Miller to knock at the door.

Then there was Stephenson, a new teacher like me. I'd noticed him at orientation. He stuck out with his starched white shirt and powder-blue tie, intent and earnest on the front row, hurriedly scribbling in a notebook as Pitts blabbed on about state requirements, basic pedagogy, and health benefits.

He looked like a minister and acted like a Boy Scout. Miller didn't like him. Unbelievably, Stephenson actually wanted to work with this crazed, attention-deficient demographic, a sentiment all of us had intoned on our applications and in interviews because that's what Pitts wanted to hear. But Stephenson meant it.

While we showed up to school in jeans and T-shirts, bleary-eyed and dreading the next eight hours, Stephenson dressed every day as if he were interviewing for a job or going to church—shirt and tie and pressed slacks, a toothy smile and a clean-shaven face. He possessed a well of energy and honeyed optimism we couldn't muster or fake.

He had a bag of tricks. No grating din percolating through the thin sheetrock that separated our classrooms, no susurrus of discontent and boredom. His classroom had life. Students' work decorated the walls: posters with timelines and collages, tests and papers displayed under a banner that read *Wall of Fame*, rules and expectations posted above the chalkboard. Students came to my class continuing debates on immigration or freedom of speech they'd started in Stephenson's class. They worried over his tests and quizzed each other nervously. They spoke about a field trip to the State Capitol. These were students who in my class sat listless and unresponsive.

With all of Stephenson's squareness and nerdiness, these students, hardened and distrusting, adored him. They sought him out before and after school, left endearing messages on his chalkboard, spoke of him without the brass-knuckled parlance of the street that usually colored their speech. They ate lunch in his classroom, stayed there long after school ended. He seemed to have a reserve of time and patience we didn't, or were unwilling to give. We disliked Stephenson in the same way we disliked the overachiever from high school, the class darling for whom the teacher has a puppy dog affection. Pitts always deferred to him in staff meetings when we discussed school improvement or classroom management. Miller would roll his eyes. Hernandez would squint and make quiet kissing noises.

I was uneasy around Stephenson and avoided him. In his presence I felt a knavish guilt, felt troubled by a reoccurring thought that maybe we could do more than babysit these kids. I told myself that after the LSAT, after my applications were in, I'd spend more time on my lesson plans, really make an effort.

In the end, I was skeptical of Stephenson. I couldn't comprehend such magnanimity for these kids, such devotion. Did he really want this, to live out his working years in a broken inner-city school? The thought baffled me.

"He's a Mormon, you know," Miller told me one night at McDuffy's. He blew into the top of his bottle. "Oh, yeah, Stephenson will tell you all about it, how he left college to do his mission in the South Side of Chicago projects, converting the same type of disenfranchised and impoverished breed who stumbles into his classroom every day. Not a coincidence that he's teaching here." Miller paused and shook his head. "He's got some romantic notion from a dozen inspiring movies about ghetto high schools. I've seen it before. They invest so much and then wake up one day to realize the world never changes. This isn't Hollywood. He'll learn his lesson and get out. These kids will break your heart, even the good ones."

I started laughing and couldn't stop.

Miller pushed his empty bottle to the middle of the table. "What's so funny? You drunk?"

Maybe I was. I suddenly had this image of Stephenson with angel wings and a halo, strumming a little harp and singing to his students in a high falsetto. He wanted to save these kids. It all made sense to me. He wanted to save these kids and really believed he could.

Pitts scheduled our parent-teacher night for the beginning of December.

All day in slacks and a starched shirt.

I waited in my classroom, pulled at the tie knotted around my neck and anticipated a rush of eager parents intent on scrutinizing their children's grades. Miller appeared in the doorway. He wore a wrinkled, white polo shirt with what looked like a hardened spot of egg yoke on the breast pocket, tucked into a pair of worn jeans he might have mown the lawn in.

"Nervous? Three years here and I've had four parents come in," he said. "I'm serious. And they want out as much as you do. *Hablas Español?*" He rapped his knuckles against the wall. "Don't forget McDuffy's after. *Muy cerveza*. And we can still catch the second half of the Suns' game."

By eight twenty-five, not one parent. I thought of slipping out the back door five minutes early and having a cold one in my hand when Miller and Hernandez walked into McDuffy's. I'd ask what took so long. They'd get a kick out of that. Then right as I was about to leave, a woman walked in.

"Mr. McClelland," she said in a thickly accented voice. She stared at the floor, practically shaking, a short Hispanic woman with a freckled face. "My son in your first period. Angel Rodriguez."

I forced a smile and pointed to a seat near my desk.

"Angel," I said, to fill the empty, awkward space between us as I pulled his grade up on the computer. "He's failing." I turned the computer screen to show her a long row of zeroes attached to Angel's name. I could've told her this without the computer. I could have, perhaps should have, told her how he bounced into class most days, every molecule of his clothes and body venting the stink of cheap weed, how he sketched in a little black notebook every day while his assignments sat untouched beside him. I could've told her this, but I needed to go. I needed to free myself of that classroom and get down to McDuffy's.

She nodded, as if she'd expected this failing grade.

"He failing all classes," she said. "I don't know what do with him." She spoke so slowly, as if she were dredging the words from the farthest corner of her mind and piecing them together. "He was in Durango for three months. He wear the bracelet on his leg after. Probation. He was good boy on probation. He'd be good boy if he on probation every day. And then after, he start trouble again, start the drugs again, start hanging out with bad friends, start with gang." She twined her fingers together. "His father have other family. He never see Angel."

I heard the clock ticking. Had three minutes passed? Had five? I wanted to get back on point. The drugs, the deadbeat father—what did this have to do with me? I wanted to be done and gone. Miller stood in the hallway, his coat over his shoulder. He pointed to his watch, made a drinking motion with his hand and then screwed up his eyes. He flipped me off and walked on.

"He can do makeup work," I said, hoping this would cheer the woman, hoping she'd nod enthusiastically and beat a quick exit. "Tell him to come in after school."

She sat solemnly, staring at the floor. "He says you his favorite teacher." And for the first time she looked at me. Her dark eyes were sad. "He say he like talking with you. Maybe you—" She stopped.

Her thin lips formed a tight smile. "Maybe you help him. Talk with him. He like you. He listen you. Tell him importance of education. Not to waste time on drugs and bad friends."

I couldn't believe it. His favorite teacher. Liked talking to me. Maybe once or twice we'd chatted about the Diamondbacks' mediocre season, whether Bob Melvin was a better manager than Bob Brenly. That was it.

What did she expect from me? What talent did I have in dealing with troubled youth? What training did I have? I didn't even have a teaching certificate. I was a teacher, barely, a teacher in title only, not a counselor or a friend or a father to these kids.

"I'll speak with him," I said, understanding I would never speak with him, understanding that this is what she wanted to hear and what would get her out of my classroom.

"Thank you," she said, her voice catching on the words. Her eyes glistened. "Thank you. God bless." And then, with bowed head, as if I might change my mind, she left quickly.

At McDuffy's, Hernandez asked why I was so quiet. His eyes darted between me and the large TV screen above the bar.

"That little mama put the moves on you?" Miller asked.

"Hell no," I said. "I was putting the moves on her." Miller slapped my back. Hernandez giggled. Above me, a series of violent collisions played out on a painted wooden floor. But I didn't care about the game.

In early February, Pitts kept hammering away in staff meetings about an increased gang presence on campus. More graffiti. The colors kids were wearing. Bandanas hanging from their pockets. What did I know? All these kids looked the same to me, all swimming in oversize pants and shirts a three-hundred-pound man could fit comfortably. We had to be vigilant, Pitts said. Someone suggested school uniforms. Pitts thought uniforms were too constraining, not enough creativity and personal expression. Parents would pull their kids from the school. We'd lose money. Someone suggested security guards. Too expensive, Pitts said.

And then it was Valentine's Day, another one of those interminable days of interruptions and unbridled merriment, kids strung out on sugar and whatever else, and in no mood to learn. I abandoned my lesson plans halfway through second period, handed out a photocopy of the state bird and told the class to color it.

Finally, the last bell rang and the school was quiet. I worked at my desk.

Law school applications were due in a week and I had to finish my statement of purpose. I was still teasing my time at that ghetto school into something meaningful, something that would lift me head and shoulders above a thousand other applicants. Pitts, with a wink, had promised a glowing letter of recommendation.

"Mr. McClelland," someone said.

Angel stood in the doorway, his twiggy body lost in a pair of saggy jeans and an oversized baseball jersey. "You think the Diamondbacks'll go all the way this season?" he asked. "You hear they're bringing Randy Johnson back?"

I didn't look up from the computer screen. I told him I hadn't, though I had. I regretted not locking the door.

"Yeah," Angel said. "They say he can't throw the heat anymore, but I don't believe it. He's gonna be like Nolan Ryan. He'll go on for years."

I wasn't in the mood. I didn't want to talk. Angel wasn't even my student anymore. He'd failed my class last semester, had never shown up for makeup work. He wasn't my responsibility.

Raul, one of Angel's friends, appeared outside the door. "Angel," he said, "They're waiting. *Vamanos*!"

Angel didn't look over his shoulder, just stared at me with his Coca-Cola-colored eyes. "My mom was really pissed off that I failed your class," he said. "I deserved it. But maybe I can make up the work. Maybe you have something I can do right now."

Raul was walking away. I could hear his voice down the hall. "Angel, *ándale*," he said.

I could have done it. Probably. It was in my power. What issue would Pitts have with a repentant student wanting to rectify a failing grade? He'd tout it as a success story. But I didn't do it. I wanted to be rid of Angel. I wanted solitude so I could finish my statement of purpose. I told him I wouldn't do it. I told him the opportunity had passed, and in that brief moment, the two of us facing each other in that classroom, I felt justified in my decision, because wasn't that the lesson Angel needed to learn? Wasn't that the tough love he needed to change his life, that all these kids needed?

He said nothing, only nodded before leaving.

I closed the door and returned to my desk. I couldn't think. I couldn't put words together. I thought of Angel, lost in those oversized pants, Angel drawing in that stupid sketchbook. I thought of his mother, kneading her dry hands together, her face a worn-out, puzzled mask.

I opened the door and looked into the hallway. Angel was gone. I walked toward the lobby, feeling a sense of urgency, but not knowing why.

The PA system crackled and Pitts's dry voice, more animated than usual, sounded through the hallway. "I need all teachers down at the bus stop on 27th Avenue. All teachers, immediately."

We walked quickly, saying nothing. Our eyes met. We smiled stupidly, as if to say, "What is it now? What insanity awaits us?" As always, we expected the ridiculous: two divas tearing out clumps of hair, wielding long painted nails like weapons, a giddy shoal of overcaffeinated teenagers shouting insults or encouragement into the fray. I looked for Miller, but he wasn't there.

And then we were running. We didn't know why. Stephenson ran beside me, tie flapping in his face, Wingtips clapping against the asphalt.

It was a brawl, fifteen or twenty boys grappling in the middle of the street. A group of students watched, jockeying for position, cell phones raised above their heads. Southbound traffic on 27th Avenue had stopped. Horns blared. People were out of their cars watching.

We pushed through the crowd toward the fight. Someone punched me in the ribs. I felt a kick to my left calf, then I heard laughter. When I looked up to orient myself, I noticed a rusted Cutlass Sierra that had once been white creep forward around a line of cars in the southbound lane of 27th. It made to pull a U-turn, then stopped in the northbound lane, parallel to the brawl. The windows were streaked and filthy. Two men I didn't recognize sat in the front seats. Raul and Angel were in the back. I stood there, wondering what they were doing, waiting for them to jump into the fight. Then the passenger window lowered and the man sitting there leaned out. I saw a thin black barrel and a wooden stock. Three quick shots, then the scream of tires.

The effect was stunning.

Students fled in every direction, as if they'd choreographed their retreat. I was knocked to the ground. The pointed tip of a high heel jabbed me in the lower back. I covered my head.

I lay there, my cheek resting against the warm asphalt. I could see tiny bits of broken glass glittering, dull seams of sun-hardened tar. My palms burned. My left calf throbbed. A little bruised, but nothing more. I felt giddy, elated. My fingers trembled with the adrenaline. I thought of what I'd tell Miller and Hernandez, how they'd want every detail of the shooting.

I got up and brushed the grit from my shirt. The street was empty except for Stephenson and some other teachers and a couple of mechanics from the garage across from the school. They stood in a circle near the sidewalk, staring down at the pavement. Their presence confused me. What were they looking at? Mrs. Phillips and Mrs. Riding, our English teachers, wept.

I walked over and saw a girl on the ground, Jackie Elzy, elfin with long black hair and dark eyes, painfully shy. I had her fall semester. Often I saw her in Stephenson's class at lunch, smiling and chatty with her friends, a side of her I'd never coaxed out. Her legs were twisted unnaturally beneath her. "It's so hot," she whispered. "It burns." And then her eyes widened. I could see the terror in those eyes, the consciousness of death.

One of the mechanics, an older Latino man with grease-stained hands, began chest compressions. At first a trickle of blood ran from Jackie's mouth and nose, and then it was like a gushing spout, blood puddling onto the street around that pile of black hair. The mechanic stopped, moved an oily hand across his forehead, and then said something in Spanish. There was a dark stain between Jackie's legs that grew until it soaked her thighs.

A hand covered my mouth—my hand—though I hadn't remembered raising it.

Cars idled past. Horror-struck passengers stared, their shocked faces absorbing the lifeless figure, the pooled blood. I knew my face must look something like theirs.

I wanted to run away and never look back, to find my car and drive. I wanted to scour Jackie from my mind forever, her inert image, those terrified eyes, scour away all the violence and thoughtlessness I associated with these kids. Let them hurt themselves, kill themselves, just as they'd always done and would always do. I didn't want to hear about it.

Stephenson stood by me, staring at Jackie with eyes that seemed to extrude from the sockets. He'd gone pale, gasped for breath through parted lips. He began to whimper like a small dog.

I took his arm, feeling a measure of distraction and purpose as I led him toward the school. He hugged his body and sobbed uncontrollably.

A group of boys had emerged from their hiding place in an alleyway and walked toward the death scene, their voices animated with the excitement. I squeezed the soft flesh of Stephenson's arm just above the elbow and spoke to him in a whisper. "They'll see you," I said. He continued to sob. "Don't let them see you like this."

I pulled him behind a white Oleander hedge and pushed him against a brick wall. "Stop," I said.

His eyes oozed. A streak of clear mucus flowed from his nose and wet his lips. "She wanted out of this," he said, practically panting. "She wanted to go to college. She wanted to be a nurse." He laid his weepy face in his palms and cried.

I grabbed at his shirt, tearing off a button just below the collar, suddenly overcome with anger. "What did you think?" I said. He'd stopped sobbing and stared at me, stunned. He had the pale face of a child. I pushed him against the brick and pressed a knuckle into his sternum until he winced. "Did you think you could change any of this? Did you think you could save them?" I felt my open hand rising, moving through the air, moving through the feeble defense of Stephenson's raised arms. I slapped his face. "Do you think this will ever change?"

I left him there, weeping into his hands.

That evening in Pitts's office, there were the statements we had to make for the police, questions to answer. What had we seen? The color and make of the car? Could we identify the passengers? The shooter?

The next night, the police arrested Angel and Raul outside a convenience store in south Phoenix. Both pleaded guilty as accomplices to second-degree murder. As far as I know, Angel never mentioned where he'd been before the shooting. Neither did I.

Regardless, the effect of Jackie's death was immediate and irreparable. Within days enrollment diminished by three-quarters. Pathway's empty hallways and classrooms hinted with their eerie silence that something horrible and unmentionable had happened. Most teachers quit. They feared the fight might come unexpectedly into the school lobby, into their classrooms. Stephenson never came back.

"Don't be a fool and quit," Miller told me. We sat in his classroom a week after the shooting. He crushed a sheet of paper into a ball and lobbed it across the room. It bounced off the wastebasket and rolled under a desk. "I mean, it's horrible what happened, this dead girl, but we're on easy street now. By law Pitts has to pay your contract until the end of the year." He smiled, hefting a thick book on real estate from his desk and then dropping it. "Hope you brought something to read."

"What about next year?" I asked. "You'll stay here?"

"Ah, my boy," he said, winking. "Don't you see? Pathway's done. Finished." Miller slid the brown, scuffed loafer from his left foot and massaged the arch. A swatch of scaly yellow skin showed through his sock's threadbare heel. "Another failed charter school. No, next year I'll be somewhere else. I hope. Who can afford to retire? At least I'll have a leg up on these wieners who quit. I'll be the guy who stuck it out to the end." He looked up from his foot. "And you? You've recently found your love of teaching, I'm sure."

"Hell no," I said. "Law school, I hope."

"That's right. Pitts was banking on that. He told me. It means something when you can tell parents that one of your teachers just went off to law school. Adds some prestige to this dump. So much for that. So much for the school. But you wait and see. Most charter schools die quietly, like a sinking ship slowly going under. Not this one. When somebody dies, it's never quiet."

Miller was right. There was blame to assign.

Jackie's family hired a lawyer. They believed the school had neglected to foster a safe environment on and near campus.

The school hired a lawyer. Months later there was some kind of settlement.

I was admitted to Stanford, a school my average GPA and LSAT scores should have disqualified me from attending. In June, the law school's dean of admissions, a man with a deep, commanding voice, a man I would do anything to become, called personally to tell me the admissions committee had awarded me a scholarship. My personal statement, he told me, had impressed them. "It sounds like you did a lot of good at that school," he said. "Changed a lot of lives. I'm sure they'll miss you."

I didn't tell him that in May the doors closed and Pathway ceased to exist.

I'm an associate in a San Francisco law firm. I live in a Spanish Mediterranean home in the Marina District. From the master bedroom balcony, I look out onto a slice of the San Francisco Bay. Often with clients, I eat at Acqua and Gary Danko.

Not long after I started with my firm, a senior partner, Jack Farrell, called me to his office. He said the firm needed a softer image. He wanted people to associate Anders, Feddersen, and Farrell with a commitment to public responsibility and community service, and to that end he'd decided the firm would make a yearly donation to Boswell Alternative High School in Oakland. But more than that, he wanted a few of us to visit the school, hand out pencils and binders, speak with the students. "You've worked with these types," he said. "You understand them." He leaned back in his chair. "This will be your project. You understand? I'm counting on you. Make us look good."

So every October a couple of associates and I visit Boswell. It's strangely familiar, the same poorly lit classrooms and graffiti-marked desks I remember from Pathway, the same sticky, dark grime covering the surface of things. The principal of the school, a short woman named Rita Gonzales, always has an assembly when we visit. She sings the praises of Anders, Feddersen, and Farrell and then invites us to say a few words to the students, something inspiring and motivating. I quote a few lines from "Invictus" and speak on personal responsibility. Isn't that what these kids need to hear? *I am the master of my fate; I am the captain of my soul.* Isn't that what might have saved

Angel and Jackie Elzy, what might save all these kids? I look out over the mass of dark faces and still feel something akin to terror.

Sitting on that stage in Boswell's dim auditorium, I always search out the teachers in the crowd, wondering if by some miracle I'll see Miller, Hernandez, or Gaines out there. "What a gas!" they'd say, yanking at my tie and grinning madly. "Look at you, counselor. Moved up in the world. But can't stay out of the jungle, can you?" For the longest time I looked for Stephenson, too. That cheesy smile. Those starched shirts. I had no ambition to teach, no real desire, no gift for it, but knowing Stephenson was out there somewhere, awing his adoring students, still believing he could save them, always comforted me. But Stephenson doesn't teach anymore.

Walking back to the office from a client lunch not long ago, I saw him get out of a cab on Howard Street, briefcase in hand, garment bag slung over his shoulder. I followed him into the Charles Schwab Building and watched him speak with one of the security guards at the information desk. He'd put on some weight and his hair had receded, but he looked like the Stephenson I remembered, except for something in the face. No smile. That annoying grin had vanished. He had on a nice suit, nice shoes. There was a thin gold band on his finger. I'm sure he had kids. I'm sure he was a good father. For a moment, I thought of saying something to him. But what? Tell him he looked well? Make a joke about how we'd gotten out alive? I said nothing, only turned and left the lobby. But if I could go back, I'd have asked Stephenson if he, too, even after a decade, still feels the needling guilt. I would never tell Jack Farrell this. I'd explain to Stephenson how sometimes at Union Square or near the Wharf, I hear them, voices booming and unabashed, their laughter piercing and irritating. Our students. I'd tell him that when I see them I cross the street.

This Same Darkness

Early Saturday morning, a man knocked at Mason's door.

Tall and heavy, the man looked damp—arms shining, shirt soaked through around the collar. He wore black orthopedic shoes with thick rubber soles.

"Name's Osborn," he said. "My daughter never came home from Seattle last night. She might've passed this way. Girl on a motorcycle. Had on a bright pink helmet."

He handed Mason a photograph.

The daughter, her hair as dark as India ink and streaked with cotton candy-pink highlights, wore a black T-shirt imprinted with a bone-white grinning skull and jagged letters that read *IMAGE COMING SOON!*

"Maybe you seen her," Osborn said.

Mason handed the photo back. "I'm sorry. My wife and I are on vacation here. We don't go out much."

Osborn brushed a hand over his eyes. "Do you have children?" he asked.

The question bothered Mason, though he didn't know why. "A hundred and fifty, September to June," he said. "I'm a high school teacher."

Immediately, Mason regretted this admission, that he was a teacher, because Osborn's wandering gaze suddenly fixed on him, as if by dumb luck he'd just happened upon the solution to some perplexing problem.

"A teacher," Osborn said. "Then you know something about my daughter. Probably had a few just like her. She's one of those independent types. Won't listen to anyone once she gets an idea in her head." He pulled a handkerchief from his pocket and wiped his forehead and the back of his neck. "I wouldn't want to inconvenience you, but maybe if you had some time this afternoon you could help me look for her. Country like this, someone goes off the road and disappears into these blackberry thickets. It's just I got these two bum knees. Can't cover much ground myself." Osborn spoke haltingly, as if leaving spaces for Mason to interrupt and agree to help.

The syrupy affectation in Osborn's voice, the long mopey face and wet puppy dog eyes, all struck Mason as too dramatic. But they weren't. Osborn was serious. He reminded Mason of one of the many neurotic, overly dramatic, overly protective parents he'd known over the years. If she were missing two days, even a day, that would be something. But hours!

"My wife and I are on vacation," Mason said again. He thought of his cup of coffee cooling on the kitchen table. "I'm sure you can understand that, Mr. Osborn. If it were an emergency, if she were hurt, I . . ."

"I know," Osborn said quickly. "It's too soon. I'm overreacting. The police seem to think so, too. They told me to wait twenty-four hours." Osborn gazed off toward the road. Overhead, a hawk climbed higher and higher on a thermal. "Let me give you this," he said, handing Mason a flier with the girl's picture. "Her name's Avery. I'll stop by this afternoon. If you're free, maybe you wouldn't mind helping."

"Sure," Mason said, knowing he'd make a point to be somewhere else that afternoon.

Osborn turned and limped down the sidewalk, rounding the corner of the house, out of Mason's sight.

There was the squeal of a fan belt and then the low popping of a bad muffler. A faded blue Suburban wheezed down the unpaved lane, gravel crackling under its smooth tires. Beads of dew shimmered on the grass. Sparrows squeaked and cut lines through the sky. Osborn's old Suburban intruded on this beauty before disappearing behind a grassy embankment. In a moment or two the sound of the vehicle rumbling down the road was lost, and everything within Mason's view, as if the natural world had agreed upon it, settled back into place.

Alone on the porch, taking in the lush greenery, Mason inhaled deeply before going back into the house, expecting the heavy morning fragrance of alder and mowed field grass. He coughed. The Suburban's exhaust still lingered in the air.

"Are you sick?" Cindy asked as Mason passed through the kitchen. She was pulling jars of strawberry jam from a pot of water on the stove.

The jam's deep crimson color blazed against the beige tile countertop, reminding Mason of something anatomical. "No. Do I look sick?"

"You look pale. Is it your stomach? You want some peppermint tea?"

"I don't want any tea," Mason said, louder and more sharply than he intended. "I just want to be left alone."

The pot of water boiled, and outside, beyond the steamed kitchen windows and beyond the cedars and alders and blackberry thickets lining the road below, a car with a noisy muffler passed. Cindy, her white apron speckled with red, stood over the stove and stared at Mason.

A deep blush crept up Mason's neck and colored his cheeks. Staring back at his wife, at her shocked expression, he felt ashamed for his shortness. He pulled a stool from under the countertop and sat down heavily.

"Somebody selling something?" Cindy asked. "Out this far?"

"No," Mason said. "Some guy looking for his daughter." Mason set the flier on the countertop and then stabbed at it with his index finger for emphasis. "She hasn't been gone twenty-four hours and he's already canvassing the countryside. He tried to enlist me in the cause. How is it," Mason asked, "that every psycho parent finds his way to me?" He ran his fingers through his hair and laughed, hoping Cindy might see the humor in what he said. "Really, it's the story of my teaching career. One after another, year after year." The temperature in the kitchen was stifling. "God," Mason said, yanking at his robe, "how can you stand this heat?"

Mason wanted Cindy to see the indecency of disturbing a man on vacation for such petty reasons. He wanted her to acknowledge Osborn's needless overreaction. He wanted to hear that this Avery Osborn, without his lifting a finger, without a single thought more on his part, was safe, would sleep in her bed that night, would embrace her father in the morning, would go off to college, marry, have children, and live happily ever after.

Cindy's eyes slid to the bottom of the flier. "Mason, this girl's missing. The man's probably going out of his mind."

Mason stood and paced the length of the counter. "I understand that." His robe clung to his back. He felt dizzy in the humid heat. "But isn't the whole thing premature? This girl isn't missing, Cindy. She probably hasn't gotten home yet. There's a difference."

"She could be one of your students," Cindy said. "Wouldn't you be concerned if one of your students didn't come home? Wouldn't you go search for one of your students?"

Mason looked down at the flier. Avery Osborn, black and white and grainy, stared back at him. Her eyes had the strange quality of following him as he paced. "Search for one lost student?" Mason laughed, a short burst to show the ridiculousness of Cindy's question. "Who would pay my overtime? I'm joking."

For most of the morning, Mason read on the back porch. First the newspaper, but the glossy back-to-school ads depressed him, a needling reminder that in two weeks he'd return to Phoenix North High School, back to his cramped, overheated classroom and the narrow, scuffed hallways vibrating with the roar of two thousand voices that every year seemed louder and more incomprehensible.

When the newspaper no longer interested him, Mason swung in the backyard hammock and read Chernow's biography of George Washington, letting the warm sun wash away any thought of Osborn and the approaching school year.

At two-thirty, when Cindy took her nap, Mason quietly gathered his wallet and keys and drove to a sports bar in Auburn called the Big Screen to watch the Diamondbacks game.

After the game Mason fell into conversation with a man sitting by him named Harris. Mason told Harris he was from Arizona, a history teacher in a Phoenix high school, and on vacation. Harris was on vacation, too, visiting his wife's family in Algona. He lowered his eyes and sighed deeply when telling Mason he was a Las Vegas parole officer in juvenile corrections. He took a pensive sip of beer and shook his head.

"Me and you are fighting the same war," Harris said. He was about Mason's age, with blond, wiry hair fading into gray and pale, freckled skin on his face and arms. The gold fillings in his molars glinted dully.

"How's that?" Mason asked.

"I know what goes on in Phoenix schools," Harris said, "because it's the same damn thing that's happening in Vegas. You can cut the apathy with a knife. White trash. *Cholos* in those silly shades and enormous Dickies. I'll be the first to admit that I'm concerned about the future of this country. In our day, we'd get the paddle if we stepped out of line. Now you can't touch these kids." Harris lifted his glass partway to his lips and then lowered it. "And you're right there in the thick of it, trying to teach them. Must be exhausting."

Had they met in a Phoenix bar, Mason would have chastised Harris for his narrow-mindedness and insensitivity, and then lectured him on the social realities of economic disparity and systemic discrimination. And Mason would have done this because as a teacher, as someone who worked with kids, that's what was expected of him. But Mason knew that in his private mind his and Harris's views weren't that different.

Mason rested his elbow on the lacquered bar and listened to the sizzle of carbonation in his bottle. "I have fifteen minutes at the beginning of class," he told Harris, "and then they're good for nothing." Mason blew into the bottle. He felt the alcohol percolating through him. "Most are lazy. But I don't worry about them. They're harmless. It's the kids who might turn on you. You can see it in their eyes. If time and place permitted, they'd shove a knife in your guts and not give it a second thought. I've learned to keep my distance."

"But I imagine you've done some good over the years," Harris said. "At least that's something. I just handhold the little shits through the system. Not much of a job. I look at grades, attendance, urine tests. At one time I cared a lot more, thought I could help these kids, silly romantic shit like that. I imagined getting Christmas cards thanking me for changing their lives. I'd never tell anyone at work that. But I know what you mean. These kids break your heart. They don't listen. They wear you down with frustration. A finger in the dike. We're that guy. How much pride can you take when that's your job?"

"The first ten years weren't bad," Mason said. He closed his eyes. "I'm proud of those years. I started a history club. We took field trips to Tombstone and Bisbee. The state gave me a teaching award. And then the white exodus out to Gilbert and Chandler. Suddenly I was teaching history to kids who didn't care. They wouldn't take notes or read the textbook. They'd quit the minute anything got uncomfortable." Mason opened his eyes and looked at Harris. "I'm supposed to teach these kids, but they terrify me."

"No chance to get out?" Harris asked. "Transfer schools?"

"Wishful thinking," Mason said. "Clean white walls and gleaming tile floors. Attentive, adoring students. A dream. Turnover at those schools is nonexistent. I'd retire before a history position opened. Plus, I'd lose my seniority." Mason smiled. "I'm stuck."

"Well, they're lucky to have you," Harris said, putting his hand on Mason's shoulder. "I know something about appearances. You're a man of education and culture. I bet you walk into that school every day knowing they're unworthy of you. You wouldn't admit that to anyone, but I know. Pearls before swine. Am I right? I respect you."

Mason smiled at his reflection in the mirror behind the bar. Harris's admiration touched him.

Driving home that evening, Mason felt renewed, as if the gloomy stain washing across his day had dissolved. The air was moist and thick and slightly chilled, and it puddled as fog in the lowest parts of the fields. In the distance, Mount Rainier's icy cap, silvery in the light of the full moon, peeked into the valley. The world seemed enchanted, and Mason felt under its spell.

He whistled and drummed the steering wheel, feeling generous and untroubled. When he saw a teenage boy in a red flannel shirt and a pair of saggy jeans, Mason slowed the car. The boy wasn't hitchhiking, only plodding along with a collapsible fishing pole in one hand and a heavy plastic grocery bag in the other, but Mason stopped the car and said, "Son, it seems you need a ride."

The boy, not saying a word, peered up the road a ways as if marking the distance in his mind and then got in the car. He stared ahead, the fishing pole on his lap, the grocery bag resting on the floor between his feet.

"Beautiful evening," Mason said. "The kind you appreciate more as you get older. At your age, I wouldn't have given it a second look."

The boy shot Mason a quick glance and then faced forward again.

"Yes, this is the kind of evening," Mason continued, "that speaks peace to the soul, that wipes away all of life's ugliness. Wouldn't you agree? An evening like this makes you feel everything's all right in the world."

"Are you a preacher?" the boy asked. "You talk like a preacher." He still stared ahead, his face shadowed, his features like stone.

"Not a preacher," Mason said, amused at the comment, "but a teacher. I teach history. What grade are you in?"

"I don't go to school," the boy said softly. Mason had to tip his head in the boy's direction to hear him.

"Don't go to school?" Mason was shocked. "What do you mean you don't go to school? Don't your parents make you? It's the law, you know."

The boy shifted in his seat, leaning slightly against the door. He gripped the handle of the fishing pole and held it tightly to his stomach. "They don't care." His voice sounded gloomy. "I'm going to be a farmer, just like my dad. He never finished school."

Mason clicked his tongue. "You know what a high school dropout earns? Most can't even support themselves, and the last thing we need is another freeloader. Have you thought about that? You have an obligation to society. For better or worse, we're all in this together." Bats darted up and down in the fields. The fence posts ticked past.

The boy folded and unfolded his arms, shifted in the seat again, and then rested his arm on the door. Mason couldn't judge the boy's height well, but he looked no taller than a jockey, a tiny, lost thing for which Mason suddenly felt a deep concern.

"Let me tell you something," Mason said. "This is the secret to success: you have to be part of a system that people value. Crime, poverty, gangs, drugs—look at people who value those systems. But education and self-reliance—they're respectable, they open doors. You see what I mean, son? A farmer isn't much at all, just a bare existence. At your age, you could be anything. Don't you want to be a doctor or a lawyer?" Mason wanted to say more. He could see a litany of words and phrases lined up in his mind: social responsibility, self-respect, self-improvement, persistence, hard work. He had an image of this disheveled boy as an adult, standing at a podium before a large crowd, hair trimmed, in a dark suit, recounting their conversation as a turning point in his life, the tough talk he needed to realize his potential.

But before Mason could continue, the boy said: "I'll get out here."

Annoyed at the interruption, Mason pulled to the side of the road. "You live here?" he asked. There wasn't a home for a mile, only a narrow gravel road blocked by a metal gate and a field with long even rows of strawberry plants that cut straight lines to the river.

"Me and my friends are camping on the river tonight," the boy said. He opened the door and stepped onto the gravel.

The boy stood for a moment outside the car, adjusted his flannel shirt, and then reached down to grab the plastic grocery bag.

"Think about what I told you," Mason said.

"Think about what?" The boy was still bent over, winding the grocery bag around his wrist, his brown hair falling over his face.

"Haven't you heard a word I've said? About being part of a system people value and respect. The day of the small farm is over." Mason looked out over the strawberry field. "Now it's all big corporations with a hundred thousand acres. Education's where it's at."

Something warm and wet struck the tip of Mason's nose and oozed onto his lower lip. Shocked, Mason turned to the boy, who glared at him. A thin string of saliva hung from the boy's sharp chin. The dome light gave his face a ghoulish appearance. Mason recoiled.

"Go to hell!" the boy yelled. "All you do is talk, talk, talk, and never listen. You don't know nothing." And with that, the boy slammed the door with a force that Mason felt in his chest.

The boy jumped the metal gate and ran down the gravel road, disappearing into the darkness.

Mason was so shocked that he sat there for several minutes, his breath coming in short bursts. The moon had risen, a large yellow skull floating above the trees, grinning dumbly down on him.

Rubbing his shirtsleeve over his lips, Mason felt that the spell had broken. The air was thick and stifling. It smelled rotten. Everything smelled rotten. Mason dabbed at his eyes and drove, hunched forward, the indigo lights on the dash and radio dial blurring.

Suddenly, a pair of flashing blue and red lights appeared in the rearview mirror, faint and distant at first and then growing brighter, approaching at a great speed.

"Damn it," Mason said, hearing the piercing scream of a siren. The blue and red lights scored the night, cut through the car, danced frenetically across the fields. Mason's heart pounded. Quickly, he pulled off the road, relieved when a sheriff's cruiser sped by in a rush of air and light.

Hands trembling, Mason drove on, squinting past the headlights to a distant spot on the road where the night seemed to be alive, blue and red lights clustering in a sphere of white light. Mason slowed. A car accident, he assumed. Able to go no farther, Mason parked on the shoulder and walked toward the sheriff's cruiser.

The deputy wore a reflective orange vest and paced nervously back and forth. A ring of keys jingled on his belt and his leather boots squeaked. Parked beyond the sheriff's cruiser were a fire truck and an ambulance, whose lights revolved silently. Two other motorists had stopped, a man in a business suit shouting into a cell phone and a young woman in shorts and running shoes who hugged her body with her arms and stared at the lights with large watery eyes. A row of burning flares threw out a vaporous pall of smoke. Mason could taste sulfur in the back of his throat.

Something was happening off the road, down a short gravel embankment, where a patch of blackberry bushes formed a dense wall of vegetation. A telephone pole rose from the green tangle. Three firefighters and two EMTs were down there, their tall shadows moving over a screen of cedars and tall alders. Every few minutes voices came over the speakers inside the fire truck.

Mason saw Osborn standing near the ambulance's open doors. A firefighter stood next to him, a hand on his shoulder, speaking softly. Mason couldn't make out the words but could see that Osborn wasn't saying anything, only nodding his head as if in agreement.

The sight of Osborn there, his wet hair spilling onto his collar, dug at something deep in Mason. He gave the deputy his name and asked if the girl was all right.

The deputy was tall, a young man with a blond, bristly mustache. He stared down at Mason. "You family?" he asked.

"Not family," Mason said. His mouth felt parched, his tongue dry and uncooperative. He wanted to hear that Avery Osborn was fine and then be on his way. "I live up the road. This morning I heard the girl was missing."

The deputy looked relieved that Mason wasn't family. He chewed his bottom lip and stared down at his boots, grinding the tip of one into the road's black asphalt. "She never made it around this corner," he said. "Slid off the road into those blackberry thickets and hit the telephone pole. Internal injuries, they told me. Her father found her about an hour ago."

"Then she's fine?" Mason asked. "She'll recover?"

The officer shook his head. "I guess I wasn't clear. She's dead. Probably died yesterday."

Mason sensed a cold numbness in his hands and feet. He looked at Osborn and imagined him limping down the road in those thick-soled shoes, his shirt soaked through, his flashlight playing over the snarl of blackberry bushes. And then that horrific discovery. *To suffer that alone*, Mason thought. And in this awareness he felt a profound gloom settle over him.

Someone shouted, "Lift," and Mason watched the firefighters and EMTs struggle up the short embankment with a metal gurney, their sweaty faces straining with the effort and shining in the bright glare of the lights. A black body bag lay on the gurney. Its contents—the outline of a chest, torso, and legs—pushed at the thin plastic.

At that moment Osborn sprang forward, his voice a dreadful howl. "Don't touch her," he screamed, blocking the gurney's progress to the ambulance. He sobbed and stared down at the body bag, his lips working mechanically but emitting no sound.

The firefighters and EMTs turned away from the gurney and

gazed off into the darkened trees. Osborn continued to sob. *Why is no one doing anything?* Mason thought. *Why doesn't someone help him?*

He went to Osborn and took his arm. "Mr. Osborn," he said. "Mr. Osborn."

Osborn turned quickly and said, "Who are you? I don't know you. What the hell do you want?" He snatched Mason by the collar. "I don't know you." A deep rumble churned in his throat.

Mason saw the thick fingers clutching his collar, the dirty, callused knuckles, the solid wrists of a man who toils with his hands. Osborn shook him, pulling him onto the tips of his toes with little effort. Mason felt the humid heat of Osborn's breath on his cheek, sensed the profound, mad sadness holding him.

Osborn sent Mason sprawling backward, arms and legs flailing, the world turning in circles. Mason felt a momentary weightlessness before he hit the asphalt and rolled once. He crouched on one knee and panted. Osborn was again at the gurney, his broad shoulders shaking as he sobbed, but the others, the fire fighters and EMTs, the sheriff's deputy and the young woman and the man holding the cell phone, stared at Mason. He thought he saw something in their gazes, not concern for him, but scorn, a silent implication that he had no right to touch Osborn, had no right to witness this man's suffering.

Mason ran to his car and drove. His cheeks burned and a rushing filled his ears. He studied the night beyond the car windows, the dimly lit houses and woody tree trunks, the square silhouettes of barns, and the great impassable blackberry thickets bordering the road.

He knew tonight he couldn't escape the darkness. Later, he knew he'd find this same darkness when he stood in the doorway of his home and heard Cindy call down to him from the top of the stairs. "That man came looking for you," she'd say. "Mason, he needed your help."

Acknowledgments

McSweeney's Internet Tendency, "A Stay-at-Home Dad Documents His Sex Life on a Fitbit—Here's What Happened"; *Bull: Men's Fiction*, "Journal of a Stay-at-Home Dad"; *Booth*, "A Letter to Daniel LaRusso, the Karate Kid"; *Monkeybicycle*, "Brigham Kimball: Mormon Missionary Extraordinaire"; *Monarch Review*, "I Reject Your Rejection"; *Grist*, "The Crossing"; *Santa Monica Review*, "Beyond the Lights"; *Silk Road Review* and *Dialogue: A Journal of Mormon Thought*, "The Righteous Road"; *Dialogue: A Journal of Mormon Thought*, "Great Heights"; *Juked*, "Lost in Furniture Land"; *The Fiction Desk* and *Hawai'i Review*, "After All the Fun We Had"; *Weber: The Contemporary West*, "Our Students"; *Concho River Review*, "This Same Darkness"